The Birth Machine

Also by Elizabeth Baines

Balancing on the Edge of the World (Salt 2007)
Too Many Magpies (Salt 2009)

The Birth Machine

ELIZABETH BAINES

CAMBRIDGE

PUBLISHED BY SALT PUBLISHING
12 Norwich Road, Cromer, Norfolk NR27 0AX United Kingdom

All rights reserved

© Elizabeth Baines, 2010

The right of Elizabeth Baines to be identified as the editor of this
work has been asserted by her in accordance with Section 77
of the Copyright, Designs and Patents Act 1988.

This book is in copyright. Subject to statutory exception and
to provisions of relevant collective licensing agreements, no
reproduction of any part may take place without the written
permission of Salt Publishing.

First published by The Women's Press 1983
Second revised edition published by Starling Editions 1996
Third further revised edition Salt Publishing 2010

Typeset in Bembo 12 / 13.5

*This book is sold subject to the conditions that it shall not,
by way of trade or otherwise, be lent, re-sold, hired out, or
otherwise circulated without the publisher's prior consent
in any form of binding or cover other than that in which it
is published and without a similar condition including this
condition being imposed on the subsequent purchaser.*

ISBN 978 1 907773 02 0 paperback

1 3 5 7 9 8 6 4 2

to my family

Once upon a time there lived a king and queen who had no children; and this they lamented very much. But one day as the queen was walking by the side of the river, a little fish lifted its head out of the water, and said, 'Your wish shall be fulfilled, and you shall soon have a daughter.'

Rose-Bud, the classic 1823 English version by Edgar Taylor of Grimms' fable, *Dornröschen* or *Briar-Rose*

One

Ladies and Gentlemen: the age of the machine.

Ladies and Gentlemen, we are proud to welcome to Boston Professor McGuirk, who has flown in from England to lecture today on the latest developments in the use of the machine.

The audience ripples. What a little guy he is. They can't see much without craning: the candyfloss tuft on his head, his gob-stopper eyeballs, lips like a twist of half-blown bubble gum. Somehow everyone expects a man of greater stature. He's a little man with a big idea. He raises his hands to quell the applause, spreading fingers like blood-specked corner-shop sausages.

When the lecture's over, will he stay for dinner? No, a taxi's waiting to take him to the airport. Back home in England his supper will be keeping warm. His wife will rescue the soup while he opens the mail: another invitation to speak; his wife will lift the phone to cancel yet another dinner-party engagement. That's the Professor; you're lucky to catch him, sometimes he's late, sometimes he's gone already when you get there; often he regrets he can't be there in any case.

His wife pours his cornflakes while he flicks through his diary. A tight schedule today. A teaching round to begin with.

'Oh isn't it today, dear, you have your rather special patient?'

'Who's that, dear?' He's taking salt with his egg. He puts the salt cellar back under the medical journal and his own latest article on the use of the machine.

'Damn!' He drops his spoon in annoyance. On the third line down a printing error seriously distorts the latest findings of McGuirk et al.

'Oh, your shirt, dear.'

'Damn the fools! What's the point of proofreading if they can still make mistakes like this in the end?'

'More coffee, dear? Everyone will understand, I'm sure. They'll see from the tables.'

'That's not the point. I ask you – in a context where accuracy is the prime consideration!'

'Your Dr Harris, dear, isn't it today that his wife is being admitted?'

Backlogs of paperwork and last-minute emergencies: in the end he's late. The students coagulate, kicking their heels in the corridor outside Ward Flora Bundy. Inside the ward the patient is prepared. The machine glistens ready. Where is he, they're all waiting, where's the Professor?

He's here – a fire door bursts open. 'Good morning, everyone, follow me, please, today we will demonstrate the use of the machine.' The students fall in and stream off behind him, jostling, not quite catching him (doesn't he get along fast for a little man?); he enters the ward and ducks into the first single room. The students fix round him like white corpuscles.

'This machine will revolutionise care on these wards. Please note that in fact what we are using here is not one machine, but two. One for controlling the drug flow, another for monitoring the progress of the patient.'

Two machines wink and glisten.

The Professor swizzles and faces the students: 'The technological leap consists in combining the two. Kindly dwell on this one moment: most medical advances have turned on just that kind of creative connection, on just that kind of leap of the creative imagination.' He waits while they dwell on it.

'This technique (ladies and gentlemen) can revolutionise lives.

'Good morning, Mrs Harris. Mrs Harris is about to benefit from our modern technology. Aren't we, Mrs Harris?' He says with a wink in Mrs Harris's direction: 'Mrs Harris is a rather special patient. How are we feeling, Mrs Harris?'

He turns back to the students: 'Now to connect the patient up to the machine.'

Are the students alert, can they catch the Professor's eye, flat blue keystone to success and qualification? Sister sets the drip up. Now take the arm of the patient. Mrs Harris's fingers are trembling just a little. What's she got to be afraid of? The Professor, professionally distant, as indeed he ought to be, nonetheless looks up and flicks another little message: Mrs Harris, above anyone, must know she's in good hands. It'll only be a prick. Flick a germ-free needle out of its sterile plastipak container. Find a suitable vein.

The Professor pauses.

'Nurse, could we have a tourniquet? Mrs Harris doesn't seem to have good veins.'

The nurse squeezes tight. The arm below the tourniquet is growing puffed and waxy. No, these veins are not at all prominent.

Everyone waits. The students wonder if they ought to feel anxious. This patient is a rather special patient. This patient doesn't have good veins.

'There. That didn't hurt, did it?'

The students relax. The patient is now attached to the machine. Press the 'On' switch; turn a button to adjust a finger on the dial. A measured amount of the drug begins to pass down the plastic tube towards the bloodstream. Place the electrodes on the two key sites on the patient's abdomen. Everything is now under control. The nurse smooths the sheet. The Professor makes a nod of professional satisfaction with a little hint of social civility, and turns away to talk to the students.

The staff nurse advises: 'Just lie back, Mrs Harris. When's your husband coming?' – over her shoulder, as she checks on everything, her pale hands hovering.

'Soon,' says Mrs Harris.

Soon.

Soon, they're telling each other up in the Centre for Medical Research, where for two hours every morning Dr Roland Harris conducts his experiments with oestrogen implants:

'Roland's late.'

'Isn't this the day his wife is going to have a baby?'

'Oh, blimey. Not today, of all days. Why didn't he tell us? The day set aside for the final bloods! Are you sure? Perhaps he's stuck in a traffic jam, the roads are up all over the city.'

The roads are up all over the city; the Victorian sewers are giving up beneath them. Ladies and Gentlemen: the age of skyscraper hospitals humming with technology above cities that crumble into the sewers.

Everything's calm. The teaching group has moved on. The nursing staff are changing over. Sister reports: Single Ward Number Fourteen. Patient Four-Five-Oh. Just arrived for induction. Mrs Zelda Harris. Harris. Special name. Special patient. The nurses grimace, and move on to the next name.

Mrs Harris lies back. A plate-glass view of the sky. Sunlight wells along the walls and makes pools on the floor. At the side of the bed, the machine hums faintly. The sky outside reels. The room floats, suspended, between the four walls.

The new Sister on duty pops her head round. Mrs Harris has her eyes closed. Is she asleep? Is she dreaming?

She opens them and looks straight back.

'That's right, Mrs Harris, have a sleep, you'll need it, that's a good girl.'

Good girl, Zelda.

And brave – not that there's anything to worry about, in the personal care of a world-respected obstetrician. Brave girl, Zelda, to overcome your own irrational fears.

Time's getting on. If they don't start soon on today's experiment up in the Centre for Medical Research, the whole trial will be lost, and with it everyone's chance of their name on a paper in the BMJ.

In cages on the walls, albino rats, mutant, twitch their bloodless tails.

Surely at least the final bloods can be done. The technician in charge unlocks the first cage. Blanched rat-noses sniff, cobweb whiskers tremble, all the colour's in the eyes – red droplets of apprehension.

It's so simple, anyone could do it, standing on their head, take off the samples and dump them in the centrifuge, but the trouble with Roland is, he likes to be there.

The technician's assistant plunges a syringe into the base of the first rat's tail.

Ten-fifty. The test tubes spun and taken out again, all in a row, the contents precipitated. Now it is time for completion of the trial. The final step in a two-month project of painstaking injection and testing of samples. Assess the long-term effects of the drug implanted, of varying levels and methods of dosage with oestrogen. Dissection, excision.

Mash up the liver and subject it to a series of chemical assays.

'What shall we do?'

'This is ridiculous.'

Still waiting for Roland.

The world is waiting for Roland's findings on the contraceptive pill.

'Can we start?'

'We can get ready. We can take out the livers.'

'Pass the chloroform.'

A new staff nurse comes in: 'How are we doing, Mrs Harris?'

Her eyes circle like moths to check the machines. She tucks the edge of the cover, and goes away.

Staff reports to Sister at the desk: 'Nothing doing.'

Sister tweaks up her breast-watch: 'Time's getting on, I'll ask Doctor to come and see if the dosage needs increasing.'

Sister brings the houseman. He looks at the chart and then back at this watch. He puts a hand on the topmost point of her belly: 'Feeling nothing just here?' It's a joke, he crinks the corners of his eyes: Just here – he nudges, to show her, this is where she's going to feel it. Sister smirks ironically.

Zelda says: 'I'm beginning to feel hungry.'

He looks away; his humour wasted, he cuts it. He turns a button and writes on the chart. He looks up, sternly, efficiently, a bank clerk finishing his calculations.

'I can promise you now something will happen. Just lie back and wait.'

'Ring your bell, Mrs Harris, when something happens.'

But nothing is happening. All she feels is hungry. If she rang, called them back, would they bring her some food?

Two

Aunties would say, staring curiously over the table: 'Doesn't she eat, your Zelda! What a lot for a little one!' – half in admiration, half in repulsion – then, lowering their voices: 'Do you think she's got worms?'

Always hungry when it wasn't convenient, too soon, or too late, waking in the night and thinking of cake. Once, overcome, she crept down in the dark, and there, under the kitchen door, a light was already shining. She pushed the door, the line of light widened to a cheese-coloured wedge: it was Father, at it before her, standing at the stove with his back turned, bulky in his shirt-sleeves and elastic braces. In his own way, on the sly, he was a bit of a cook. The coals hissed. Something was sizzling on the hotplate.

He said without turning: 'What in hell are you doing here?'

She said, 'I'm hungry.'

He snorted. The thing on the hotplate whispered.

'What are you making?'

'Toast.'

She came and peered. 'That's not toast.'

'Call it what you like. I call it toast.'

The slice glistened on the stove, deep yellow, emitting tiny bubbles at its lower edges. She saw he'd done something new: buttered the bread first, before cooking. He did another for her, turned the loaf on its end and sawed across flatwise.

'You'll cut your thumb,' she warned.

He laughed. The knife zig-zagged towards the corner where his thumb hovered, waiting, a hard plum with its elongated dimple. The blade came through, his familiar thumb caressed it. He slapped on butter, and threw the slice on the stove.

The toast was moist, with a charred green taste. He'd been working on the table, and it was scattered with his drawing things – set squares and compasses, strange spiky instruments. She dropped black crumbs on the papers and brushed them off, leaving greasy mottlings.

'Are those patterns, or maps?'

He saw the stains she'd made and screwed up his mouth as though a gooseberry had lodged on his tongue. He said: 'Get to bed.'

She went, wondering: Where had he got it, his wet-toast recipe? From the place far away where he lived as a child? Or had he just made it up himself?

Upstairs, Mother, the real cook, lay fast asleep unawares. Zelda crept in beside her, and her adult body stirred closely, giving off a faint odour of ripe fruit. By day she was changed to a different creature: a quick-moving conjuror of winking juices, a wizard whose touch made herbs grow up in green puffs every summer by the garden wall where the other village children sat and kicked, releasing scents and calling to Zelda, their pockets bulging with sweets, lollipop sticks poking out of their faces.

'Want one, Zelda?'

She put out her hand.

Hey presto, there was Mother behind her, coming out to pick sage for dinner. 'No, she doesn't want one, she doesn't want to spoil her dinner.'

Zelda dropped her hand again. The children slavered and chewed, convulsed their jaws over toffee. Mother picked beneath them, irritated, tight-lipped, snapping off the plant heads. 'Move your feet, please.' The children swung their legs up. 'Off you go, she isn't coming, it's nearly time for dinner.'

Faggots for dinner. Mother rolled her sleeves up. 'Pass the sage.' Zelda passed the bundle, furry as an animal, and Mother brought the knife down. The leaves bounced, she trapped them, dragging them back again, she chopped with such vigour the whole table shuddered, she reduced the lot to black rubbery shreds. No mercy. Now the liver: the dark mass shivered as she scooped it, little tongues of it licked her wrist. She pushed it into the mincer, it choked, she churned hugely at the handle, and slapped back the little arms that flailed; purple bits flew off and stuck like leeches. The air was filled with the high metallic stink of blood.

But then abracadabra, the dish was in the oven, and Mother flicked a cloth, whisked away every sign, and the smells began to turn warm and rich. At last, the finished product emerged: transformation; aromatic faggots.

There wasn't enough for seconds; the pot was empty. They all sat back. Before they'd emptied their mouths, the kids could be seen through the window, waiting on the wall again, blowing giant pink bubbles and popping them.

'Disgusting,' said Mother. 'Don't their parents feed them?' She appealed to Father who was picking his teeth: 'Have you seen the dirt round that Hilary's neck?' and then said, turning to Zelda: 'It wouldn't surprise me if she has head lice. Don't put your head too close to hers, Zelda.'

The den in the wood was made with blankets from Hilary's. Light twitched through its moth holes. They crouched inside, Zelda and Annie in charge of Hilary's little brother. Hilary had gone off to look for more branches. The little brother was snivelling.

Annie rolled her eyes. 'What's she got to bring him for?' She turned, whipping her pigtails, and said to him sharply: 'Shut *up*, little boy!'

The little boy roared.

'Ignore him,' she said then, tightening her lips up.

The little brother tugged his shirt front, bunched it up to his nose, and stuck his thumb in.

'Thank goodness for peace,' she said to Zelda with a sour tone but a look of satisfaction on her pale beaky face. Then, sweet as plum pudding: 'Want to come a lickle walkie?'

The small boy glared scorch marks. She stuck out a hand, stiff like a puppet. He let out a wail.

She turned away in disgust. 'Little brat. What's the use of bringing babies?'

As she spoke, a boom came out of the distance. The little boy stopped crying, his mouth hung open. Beyond the woods, over the meadows, workmen with lorries were blasting. The little boy's chin began to tremble.

They could do without babies.

Saucepans they could do with. They could furnish the den. They needed utensils.

'Bring a saucepan, Zelda.'

'Can I have a saucepan?'

'What for, I'm busy.'

The cookbook lay open on the kitchen table. A guest was expected, a colleague of Father's. Mother was cooking roast beef with marjoram.

'That's a healthy piece of meat,' said Father, giving it a pinch in passing. It sat on the dresser, jewelled and plump in a yellow crust of fat.

Zelda leaned on the table, her nose in the cookbook.

'You're in my way!' said Mother. She edged aside, still reading: *Skewer the meat to enable the flavour of the herb to penetrate.* She looked up and checked: Mother was jabbing, her fleshy arms wobbling, and the fat around the meat became pocked with rows of deep holes, each hole somehow shocking and filled with pink light.

The guest arrived, a stiff round man with shiny shoes, and sat with Father, waiting for food. Zelda hung in the doorway. 'Have you seen the plans?' Father was asking. They grinned, heads together, swigging whiskey.

Mother brought in the meat, red-faced, hair askew after all her preparation. But it was Father who did the carving. He flexed his deep-marked thumbs and the beef rolled off in tongues.

'Oh yes,' said the visitor, as Father was carving. 'I'm sure there'll be no problem, the plans will be passed.'

Father balanced the slices on the blade and passed them.

They all tasted. Was it good, was it subtle? (*Marjoram*, said the cookbook, *in too great quantities can be overpowering.*) Mother smiled. Yes, just right, a warm hint, a suggestion.

As they ate, from out of the distance came the sound of blasting.

Three

ELEVEN O'CLOCK. The Professor faces his audience of students. The students are alert to assess if the lecture will dispense with the need to read the textbooks. At any rate, it's bound to be an easy lecture to follow: the Professor is renowned for shaping his lectures into well-defined headings, every one of which he'll make a point of writing on the board.

He begins, takes the chalk, and turns away from them and scratches. His blue suit flickers in front of what he's writing, they can't see yet what it is. The keenest among them fidget with their pencils poised. The Professor stands back to reveal the heading: INDUCTION OF LABOUR, and at the same time he says it out loud. The students start scribbling.

The Professor says clearly: 'This is defined as an attempt to imitate labour before the time it would have occurred spontaneously.'

He reins them along, as they scribble, away at the end of the sentence. He turns and writes while they get there: INDICATIONS FOR INDUCTION OF LABOUR. He makes the first of the heads of two columns: OBSTETRIC.

Now he elucidates. 'Obstetric. Any condition may be an indication if it is considered safer for the mother, or for the foetus or both, that the pregnancy does not continue any longer. In practice the most common indications are . . .'

The horizontal headings begin to be supported by vertical lists like classical Greek columns. The students warm to the pattern of it. The sun comes in through the lecture-room window and makes the Professor's auburn hair a halo.

Eleven o'clock. Mrs Harris rings her bell. A student nurse goes to answer.
'Could I possibly have something to eat?'
The student doesn't know. She goes away to ask someone else. She bumps into Staff. Can Mrs Harris have something to eat? Staff looks doubtful. A snack is permissible in the early stages, as long as there's no likelihood the patient will need an anaesthetic . . . Staff goes off to ask Sister. Now where's Sister got to?
Sister's in her office, having her tea break. Zelda's strapped to her bed. In spite of everything, Zelda's hungry. Roland's somewhere in the city, his red car winking. In the Centre for Medical Research they are getting ready to do the livers.

Eleven-five. A West-Indian staff nurse. 'Hallo, dear,' she calls as she enters, as though she's recognised a friend across a crowded street, someone else, not Zelda. She checks the machines, lightly touches the bottle of solution; her butterfly fingers rest on Zelda's pulse.
'Your husband coming soon?'
'Oh yes,' says Zelda. 'Yes, soon.'
'That's right,' says the staff nurse, 'plenty of time anyway, nothing happening just yet.' She smiles with teeth that seem lit from inside; her body springs on her legs, ready for flight, or for action. She laughs lightly, carelessly, and steps away, out of the room.

The students write industriously, those getting on best who've developed a personal shorthand. This is turning out to be a comprehensive lecture. Now the subdivisions make diagonal inroads across the classical arrangement.

The Professor is dealing with POSTMATURITY. This is a condition he defines as that of the foetus where it is at risk due to prolonged pregnancy. He is discussing the changes which may be expected in this condition, and is now on DECREASE IN PLACENTAL EFFICIENCY.

'In the average forty-week pregnancy the placenta reaches its maximum efficiency about the thirty-sixth week, after which time there is a steady decline in its ability to function . . .'

Arleen Manning, winner last year of the Joshua Goodfellow Memorial Prize, holder of a commendation in the First MB, sitting now in the front row of the lecture theatre, gets nudged in the elbow. Rick Jenkins, a failure from the previous year, heading for failure a second time over, signals that his biro's given up, does she have a spare? She frowns with irritation and fumbles for one quickly, she doesn't want to miss the next bit; with relief she gets it down:

'– so that the older a placenta is, the more senile it becomes, and the more inadequate to nourish the foetus.'

Everyone waits for Mrs Zelda Harris, on a constant infusion, to begin her first uterine contraction. The nursing staff wait. They write in the notes: *Eleven-ten. No contraction.* Mrs Zelda Harris half-lies, half-sits, her legs splayed, her buttocks tingling from sitting so long in the same position, her belly doming the bedclothes. Within lies the placenta, past its maximum efficiency, no longer rich in a nourishing blood supply. Something shifts, under the bedclothes, beneath the wall of her uterus. The foetus stretching and waiting. Nothing else. No contractions.

Everyone waits. Zelda waits. Waits for bread and jam. Waits for her husband. Up at the Centre for Medical Research a lab technician takes a pin and drives it through the pale pink palm of the first rat for dissection. The rat lies, cruciform. Inside is the liver, which will reveal the new truth, and provide the world with scientific data. With his plastic-gloved hand, the technician pinches up the warm belly skin and makes a curt snip. He cuts a neat line towards the chin. He cuts four diagonals. He pins the skin back in two aprons. The organs nestle in their gleaming tissue package. The heart is still throbbing. Now to snip the connective tissue. A steady hand at this stage: one slip now and blood would get everywhere, a mess that would alter the balance of everything, the expected results, and the hopes of everyone. The heart shudders; its contents start to congeal.

A flea crawls out from the cooling neck fur, stands poised on its surface, then leaps away.

Annie grabbed the saucepan and hurried away.

'We got it, we got a saucepan! Now we can cook, we can make a stew.'

In the den, she stirred it: herbs from the garden, weeds from the wood. 'Delicious! Now be patient while it cooks – get back!' she snapped at Hilary's little brother perched on the doll's pram in the den. She pinned him back again. 'There, that's Mummy's good baby, there-there, in a minute lovely stew will be ready to make his lickle legs grow big and strong.'

His legs already sprawled so far over the pram sides that his feet scraped the floor. Everyone giggled. He didn't like that, he struggled to get off and the pram rocked madly.

'Stop it!' spat Annie, and shoved him in the chest.

He started to cry.

'Horrid ungrateful little boy, when Mummy's been so busy making tasty stew for him!' She shoved again.

'Leave him alone,' said Hilary.

'Well, he's useless! He keeps moving!'

She stood back and the little boy climbed down.

She swiped the doll off the floor. Its striped arms and legs spun circles. She jabbed it in the pram. Its face peered out with a startled expression.

The doll was better.

'There, *what* a patient baby, waiting quietly for her lovely stew! She's very lucky – you're all very lucky, not everyone who gets such stuff, no wasting any when you get it, mind!'

They all sat and waited.

'Baby first.' She spooned the stew at the doll. Green dribbles ran down its chin.

There was a noise, a sharp crack, outside, beyond the blankets. They all heard it and froze: a twig snapping.

Silent, fingers to lips, they crouched to the entrance. A boy was standing there watching as they crowded and peered.

He said, curious, challenging: 'What are you doing in there?'

'Mind your own business.'

He threw a stone, quick as a lizard. Everyone flinched.

Annie said quickly: 'You can play if you like, we're having our dinner.'

'There's no room,' said Hilary, sullenly, angrily.

'Yes there is,' snapped Annie. It's delicious, come and taste.'

The boy looked doubtful.

'Come on!'

Freckled face first, the boy came into the den.

'Here!' She offered a spoonful. He was suspicious. He sniffed and wrinkled his nose. She encouraged: 'It's lovely, we've all had some, haven't we?' They darted reptile looks from one to the other, sharing the lie. He looked up and saw their expressions.

'No thanks, it's revolting.'

'Ahah!' said Annie quickly. 'Lucky you didn't fall for it. It's a spell!'

Now he was interested.

The Professor is up to METHODS OF INDUCTION. Sub-heading One: MEDICAL. Here he discusses the posterior pituitary extracts, the hormones employed in induction for their action on the uterus (they are much more powerful it seems, than, for instance, castor oil, traditionally used for this purpose – and naturally, therefore, superior and more desirable). He talks about administration: he doesn't favour tablets, oral administration doesn't give the doctors anything like the kind of control that is obviously desirable; what he recommends, what is now recommended, is continuous intravenous infusion (a method helping to avoid the dangers of these hormones – in the main, excessive stimulation of the uterus).

He concludes the section: 'These hormones are now available in purely synthetic form.'

Eleven-thirty. Zelda lies back, her stomach empty, a pure infusion passing into her bloodstream, developed by pharmacologists, distilled in a laboratory, labelled and coded. When she moves her arm the whole contraption shakes, and the liquid taps and glitters. Synthetically pure. Innocuous-looking as water.

They should strengthen the spell. A snail bobbed, woodlice flickered. Stir thirteen times, thirteen unlucky, unlucky for some.

The live things went down and came up again.

It had gone very quiet. Outside in the wood the birds had stopped singing. What was the spell for? They hadn't decided. Somewhere in the distance an engine was roaring.

They're long past INDICATIONS: they're almost concluding METHODS – MEDICAL. The Professor sums up:

'The method of induction most widely used now, and generally found to be both safe and satisfactory, is a constant infusion of oxytocin preceded by an enema and low amniotomy.'

This brings him on to Sub-heading Two: SURGICAL.

No one has cut her any bread and jam. Bread and butter would do, or even bread and margarine. Though cake would be nicest.

'All right, Mrs Harris, you can have one slice.'

Not cake.

An old woman was making cake. They could smell it as they passed her cottage. They scuttled up and crouched behind her garden wall. As they peeped, she came out to the dustbin, shuffled down the path in their direction. They knew her, they'd seen her around, she wore a tea-cosy hat and boots that flapped at her ankles. They bobbed out of sight. The metal lid clanged on the afternoon air. All around was the warm brown smell of baking.

'Hello, my pretty darlings,' she said.

They looked round, shocked. She couldn't see them, surely. They looked from one to the other.

'That's right, my darlings,' she said again, turning away, talking to no one. They knew then; a sure sign.

Up on the ridge tiles of the cottage a line of dark birds sat, turning this way and that, with steely feathers, clockwork. Their beaks opened with clicks. They cocked their bird-heads.

The children crept away on their haunches, escaped. They had not been taken in by the ginger-parkin smell.

When they got back, the doll was just as they'd left her,

magically protected. But what a mess, all that food on her face!

'Clean her up, Nurse, come and clean the baby princess!'

Zelda spat on her skirt and wiped the doll's face.

'There!' said Annie. 'Now she's lovely. Well, she's bound to be lovely, a princess promised by the fishes.'

They stared. But then, of course, they all remembered, they knew: the fairytale that began with a fish, bringing a promise, breaking upwards through the surface of the water.

'Amniotomy,' announces the Professor: 'Artificial rupture of the uterine membranes. If the forewaters are ruptured, this is called low amniotomy. If the hindwaters are ruptured, this is called a high amniotomy.'

Arleen Manning translates this into her personal shorthand, which gets it down quickly but preserves the verbal reasoning for the purpose of the exam.

'Both methods depend on the principle of reducing the volume of the uterine contents by drawing off some of the liquor. This initiates contraction of the uterus.'

Who didn't know about that, a fish flexing, jumping through a ring in the water, opening its mouth and casually, confidently promising a daughter?

'Oh, but she's lovely,' said Annie, rubbing noses with the doll, 'lovely-lovely-lovely. Just as all the fairies of the kingdom promised.'

'Don't forget,' said the boy, wanting to be in on it, 'don't forget the thirteenth fairy's promise.'

Four

EARLIER THAT MORNING she shivered in the hospital corridor. A new admission for induction of labour.

Nine o'clock on a Monday morning in January, in the early nineteen-seventies. The age of technology, and resulting creeping unemployment, the age of strikes and shortages and economy measures. The heating turned down all over the hospital.

The floor shone coldly, off into the distance. Her ankles, naked above her slippers, felt bony and brittle. Her clothes were tied in a black plastic dustbin bag on the floor beside her. A nurse came out of a side door. Brown uniform: auxiliary. 'Give me those,' she said dourly. She held out her hand for the plastic bag. She took it, expressionless, and went away. After a while, she came back without it. 'Come in here, please.' She disappeared behind a plastic curtain. Zelda stood up and followed.

Behind the curtain was an examination bed. At a trolley beside it the nurse was unpeeling plastic gloves from their paper packing, slipping her hands in, and sloughing off the paper. 'Get on the bed,' she said, without looking round.

Zelda clambered up, heaving, stumbling over her own bulk, getting her gown caught. She took the weight of her body on the bones of her elbows, and levered herself onto her back. The nurse turned now; she had a razor in her hand. She moved forward impassively and began to shave her. The razor slapped, coldly, briefly. The job was done. The nurse turned away. Zelda moved her legs, and the hairs, not shaved closely, rasped and prickled. 'Turn on your side,' said the nurse, coming back. She heaved round, and received the cold intrusion of the enema.

Everything was cold. The sides of the bed as she lumbered down again, the white-tiled wall, the lavatory seat. 'Good girl,' they said, as she emerged from the lavatory. They took her elbows, one each side of her, and led her up the passageway. Another bed like a table, in a room little more than a corridor. Their uniforms rustled: dun overalls of nylon. The faint smell of sweat trapped inside the synthetic fabric caught her nostrils as they reached across to help her. The plastic sheet on the bed crackled. 'Wait here,' they said. 'Someone will come.'

She shivered. Her view was the ceiling and the upper parts of the walls. All was painted mute green: pipes ran along the corners between ceiling and walls, also green, painted over. High up, a small window showed a patch of the sky. From far away, low down, came traffic sounds. Roland should be on his way by now. A white clock on the wall told the time: nine-thirty. At the end of every second, the big hand clicked forward.

The mound of her belly hid the view of the door. She thought of Roland's car nosing over the intersection on the south side of the city, edging up the slip road, inside the windscreen his wire-rimmed glasses flashing right and left, then nipping quickly: was he safely across?

He'd said before she left, his glasses blinking doubtfully: 'Do you want me to come with you? Or shall I come on later?'

He watched her packing her case. Two nighties, a pair of slippers. Something to read – *would* she read, would there be time for reading?

He said: 'I don't suppose there's much point me coming for the first hour, anyway.'

'No,' she said, 'I'm perfectly capable of going alone – I mean, it's not as if I'm *ill* is it?' She laughed.

'Or even in labour,' she added. And laughed again.

He didn't laugh. She decided he must be anxious, and she kept on laughing, to reassure him.

Lying on her back was the most uncomfortable of all. It ached, and her belly rested on her like a lump of lead. If she lifted her head now she saw dud rubber and metal: the corner of a machine. The clock clicked on: nine-forty-five.

A noise in the corridor caused her to struggle onto her elbows. A young doctor stood in the doorway. He wore a cap and gown of surgical green. She glimpsed white rubber boots and a bucket in each hand. Before she collapsed back, she registered that his ruddy face was widely grinning.

His face swam up over the horizon of her belly. She smiled back. He caught her eye, he looked surprised. It wasn't her he'd been smiling at. But he was jolted to speak: 'Sorry to keep you waiting,' and he tucked her heels up and swung her knees open. He bent away and clanged a bucket down below the table. She couldn't see him now. She swung her head sideways and saw around her belly that he was busy with his back to her at the far end of the room. There was the sound of rustling, of soft plastic tissue, then the clang of something metal. His face appeared again, between her legs. 'Just relax,' he said, not looking at her face, concentrating on his task. The top of his cap dipped away. A plastic-glove touch on her vulva; immediately, suddenly, cold metal inside her. The clock on the wall said, Cluck. Then a pain, too buried to be sharp, but a sense of everything pinched together: her womb, her guts, her knotted spine.

The doctor drew back. She heard a clatter, like heavy raindrops in a metal trough, then the fluid gobbed into the bucket. And kept on falling. The doctor wandered away. Only the sound of it. No sensation. Body temperature, pouring out unfelt. The doctor came back and changed the bucket, and the water clanged into its emptiness.

He popped round her belly: 'All right then?' He was looking straight at her now, almost smiling. A nurse's voice came from the door: 'Finished in here, Doctor? Number three's ready.' 'Right,' he said, wiping his hands on a towel, and gave Zelda a nod, and was gone. She lay spreadeagled, water trickling now, the sound petering out.

A sensation began: a tight band round her abdomen. The wall-clock hands reached ten o'clock. Two nurses in waxy brown came in through rubber side doors that yielded like flaps of skin. The buckets were removed; she was wadded, her gown pulled down. A hospital porter pushed through the doors with a trolley. Black rubber loomed towards her head; the trolley thudded through. Walls skimmed past at close quarters; sharp corners swerved, then swung away again. They stopped at lift doors. The porter peeled them aside. The small ceiling blinked bright yellow and the lift walls throbbed and hummed. Out again, and straight through to the ward: Flora Bundy, Single Room Number Fourteen, the room with the machine. They lifted her across, and tucked her in, and went away.

She curled back the sheets and swung her legs out and stood. Her knees wobbled. A flood of water rushed down her legs and spread across the floor. Now she did feel it, its tickling warmth on her cold feet. The pool spread and shone across the vinyl. At once Sister came in.

'Mrs Harris! What on earth are you doing out of bed?'

'I want to go to the lavatory.'

'Then I'll bring you a bedpan. No getting out of bed once your waters have been broken. We can't risk an infection. Naughty girl, now, Mrs Harris!' She smirked, making a joke.

'You just sit still there.'

Another clock, also white. It said: Chock. Ten-ten.

Zelda sat propped on pillows, her hands folded on the sheet.

The sheets and pillows were grey, these days no longer boiled, but steeped in disinfectant distilled in some industrial laboratory, a process which leaves them antiseptic but grey.

The nurse came back with a cardboard bedpan, and left with it discreetly covered with paper. 'Professor McGuirk will be along in a minute,' she said over her shoulder as she went through the door.

Ten-fifteen on a January day in the age of paper towels and disposable bedpans and easy-care laundry techniques. Zelda lay on grey pillows and waited. Patient girl, Zelda.

An auxiliary came in with a mop and sullenly slopped it in her puddle. She looked up, once, to move the bedside cabinet out of the water, a glare that avoided contact with Zelda. What a mess. Bad girl, Zelda.

Five

'YOU SHOULDN'T HAVE done it.'

Mother sat on the doorstep in the early summer, shelling peas and delivering admonitions and warnings.

She was in the way. 'I'm coming through there in a minute,' called Father.

Mother's stockingless legs lay loosely staked across the entrance, the bone-lines sheeny in the sunshine, the undersides wobbly.

She took no notice of Father, and kept on at Zelda, all the time shooting peas with her thumb, rattling them off into the metal bull's-eye of the colander.

'Don't you ever go playing by the river again. I'm amazed at that Hilary, you'd think she's old enough to know better than to take you, she must be nearly thirteen.'

Mother stopped shelling.

'She's a very odd girl. She doesn't act her age. Why doesn't she play with the girls her own age?' A look of sly suspicion crossed her face as she sat there.

Then suddenly she began again, snapping the pods and sending the peas spinning like fairground marbles.

'Watch out!' called Father, warning them to move.

'Zelda, stop eating peas, they're too expensive to waste so early in the season – it's not as if they're any decent size.' She considered: 'Perhaps I should have cooked them in their pods.'

Father advanced. 'What do you think,' she asked him, 'should I have cooked the peas in the pods?'

Father tried to step over; she swung her legs as he lifted his foot, and his big square frame swayed and almost fell.

'Bloody hell, woman, couldn't you see I was stepping over?'

'Sorry,' she said. 'Sorry. What about the peas? Do you like them mange-tout?'

Father scowled: 'You know what I like. Do you want to break my neck?'

'Oh, good,' said Mother, swinging her legs away. 'Just as well I shelled them.'

Zelda ran off. Mother called, 'Remember, no going to the river!'

There was a world of brown light beneath the surface of the river. A log lay in a sandy trough. Dark forests waved. Look, the log was alive: a shutter lifted and tipped; the fish fixed you with his eye. His jaws grinned. He stared, unblinking. Knowing. What was it he knew? His grin widened, satirically, as a cloud of small fish-shadows drifted over his back. The cloud started, then disappeared amongst the weeds. The big fish had gone.

From higher up the bank, the sun made a tight white skin on the water. They climbed towards the field.

'Get down!' hissed the boy.

They didn't know what for, but they dropped on their bellies. Hilary grabbed her little brother. The boy signalled for silence. The little brother, wondering too much to protest, strained his neck to look from one to the other. Why were they hiding? They could see nothing through the grass. They moved their heads this way and that and the blades slipped from side to side. A black beetle crawled out near Zelda's hand and twitched its antennae. The calves of Hilary's thick legs bulged above her wrinkled socks. The little brother started to struggle. They raised themselves onto their elbows. Then they saw it: a bright purple dot disappearing over the hill. Were they stalking? Or simply hiding? In order to know, they looked at the boy.

'Come on!' He darted forward, crouching, beckoning them to follow. They stood. At that moment a fish jumped out of the water.

Look!

A real fish jumped. Punched its nose through the surface, gaped for a second, and then slipped back down.

It was there, you could see, widening ripples from the place where it happened.

'Come on!' The boy was impatient. They raced over the hill. It was the old woman. She was going down the hill in her purple tea-cosy hat. She skirted round the field, into the lane, and reached the cottages. They followed, at a distance. She turned into her gate. She looked back and saw them coming. It was too late to hide. She stood and waited with her hands on the gatepost. They slowed, but the little brother ran on.

'What a pretty little boy!' they could hear her saying. She put her hand on his head. Her fingers were purple and bladdery, with yellow nails.

'Would he like some sweets?' she asked the others as they approached. 'Would you all like a sweet?' Her eyes were small and filmy in her hanging leathery face.

That was another warning: never accept sweets from ugly strangers. They put out their hands, suspiciously. Her blobby fingers brushed their palms. They withdrew them quickly, clutching tiny crinkly packages.

Inside the den they unwrapped them. Liquorice toffees. They sucked the corners. The taste, at least, was all right. They looked at each other and waited for things to happen, for faces to grow pale and for hands to clutch stomachs. Nothing did. They relaxed, and started chewing.

'That's OK then,' said Annie. 'That means the baby princess can have some.'

She took the sticky lump out of her mouth and pressed it against the doll's round one, then popped it back in her own and wiped her hand on her dress. She laid the doll down and pulled up the pram hood. 'Mummy's baby has to get some sleep now.' The doll's white face, smeared with black, loomed in the shadow. Thin black outlined the corners of their mouths. They all grinned, with black teeth. Annie rocked the pram smugly. No one else's evil could touch them.

So what was the fish, Zelda wanted to know, that had jumped from the river? What was the name of it? The boy and Hilary argued. The boy said he was right, he ought to know, he went fishing with his Dad, his Dad told him the names. How could he know, said Hilary, he didn't even see it. And Hilary was older, she was nearly thirteen.

Annie rocked the doll, smugly out of the argument, rocking the baby the fishes had promised her.

But the real fish had been silent. The real fish knew better than to make any promises.

It is not as expected. Mrs Harris should have started in labour by now. Eleven-forty-five. Nearly hospital lunchtime. Along the hospital corridor a porter steers his trailer of cupboards and a hundred hot dinners. The cases clatter and shunt as he stops at the ward. Auxiliary nurses clang the steel doors open and help him slide out the metal trays.

Nothing for Single Room Number Fourteen. Not for someone who ought to be in labour by now.

The houseman clicks his heels at the bottom of her bed. 'Well, Mrs Harris, are we being stubborn?' Come on, smile, Mrs Harris.

'Mm,' says Doctor. He considers, his head cocked. He

puts his hands each side of her belly, as though he's about to lift it off her: 'Didn't we say you'd felt something?'

'No,' says Zelda.

'Yes,' says Sister.

Zelda looks at Sister.

Sister says to Doctor: 'She had a contraction immediately after the amniotomy.'

Zelda's looking at Sister.

Sister turns to Zelda: 'The pain you said you felt immediately after your waters were broken.'

'Oh yes,' says Zelda, 'but that went away again.'

'Mm,' says Doctor to Sister: 'Spontaneous labour. In view of that, she's very slow to respond.'

Zelda looks at Doctor. Zelda looks at Sister.

Sister's nodding. Doctor and Sister look at each other.

Doctor turns to the machine. 'Well, we'll increase the dosage again. Something will happen, Mrs Harris.'

They were strengthening the spell, using herbs from the garden. The sun was hot in the sky. They leaned over the wall when Mother wasn't looking and grabbed handfuls of marjoram that was bushing now, striking up with long reddish stems; in a week or two it would flower, pale-purple and powdery.

The boy came running to meet them. 'Have you seen what they're doing the other side of the hill?'

They took no notice. They were busy. They made up the field with their bundles; the boy followed. When they got to the top of the hill they could see for themselves. Overnight, it seemed, the land was gashed open. Diggers and lorries crawled about in the distance like earwigs. They were extending the road.

'My Dad says,' said the boy, 'it's the road to the power house they're building down the river.'

'What's a power house?'

Mother rubbed lard in flour. 'Where they make electricity.'

'How do they make it?'

'Ask your father. He knows.' Too busy for questions, she rubbed her hands and filled the air with a cloud of fine flour.

They sat in the den. The blasting sounded, an underground gong.

'My Dad says,' said the boy, 'it's bound to bring jobs to the village.'

Annie bashed the herbs in the pot. Marjoram, said the cookbook, for the easing of the spirits.

Six

'HERE YOU ARE, Mrs Harris, you can have a cup of tea! Mrs Harris!' The nurse shakes her. 'All right, Mrs Harris? Were you asleep? What were you dreaming?' The nurse looks knowing. Of course we all know what Mrs Harris will be dreaming. We won't be long now.

Midday. The hands of the clock bang the moment into place.

'Sister says you can have a cup of tea.'

There, Mrs Harris, after all you can have something!

In Sister's office Doctor tells Sister about his suspicion in Mrs Harris's case of Primary Inertia.

'Ah,' says Sister.

They fall silent.

He bends and fiddles with his bleep. Sister notices the tiny black curls lying flat on his neck. Doctor looks up. Sister tidies the files. Doctor sees Sister's left hand is naked of rings.

'We'll have to wait, though,' says Doctor, 'and see what happens in the next half-hour.' He suspends his judgement on Mrs Harris's uterus. But he's keeping it ready.

Sister is impressed by Doctor's acumen.

Doctor asks her: 'What time do you get off duty?'

Across the road the students spill out of the School of Medicine. Arleen Manning is first, briskly stepping into cold bright daylight. Ahead, the glass walls of the maternity hospital tower and glitter. A purposeful breeze strikes across the Medical School steps. Arleen Manning, in high-heeled boots and a coat of the latest maxi fashion, clutching her ring folder, once more finds Rick Jenkins plucking her elbow. She sighs. She's off to get a quick lunch and then a spell in the library before the two-hour clinical this afternoon. She doesn't want to end up burdened with him.

Rick Jenkins says anxiously: 'Arleen, did you get the last bit? It was awfully rushed, wasn't it? I'm not sure I got it all down right: do you think I could borrow your notes to compare?'

She answers contemptuously: 'I'd like to look at them myself first.'

She strides away across the courtyard, her bobbed hair making quick little flips in the wind. She's blowed if she'll give a lift-up to a dunce like him. As if he could interpret them: her notes snuggle under her arm, cryptic, condensed to the essence of thirty-five lectures, but with the power, at the touch of her eyes alone and her remarkable memory, to unfold to thirty-five three-thousand-word essays. She swings her other arm and marches up the steps of the library, changing her plan in order to shake him – she's not hungry, anyway.

The librarian smiles at her familiar face. Arleen passes into the reading room to rewrite neatly the final section of the lecture, intact but rushed and therefore untidy: FOETAL MONITORING.

Back on the top floor of the Medical School, in the Centre for Medical Research, Dr Roland Harris's technicians are breaking for an early lunch. The liver assay is well under way now, the livers lie in separate jars, carefully coded. The technicians put their outdoor coats on. Should they grab a quick sandwich in case Roland turns up soon, or could they risk a pizza?

On Flora Bundy Ward they are giving out the dinners. Each bed has a tray on wheels that slips right across it like a giant paper clip. The dinner goes on the tray. Which dinner for which bed? In these days of improved mass-catering techniques, there's a choice of menus – as long as you fill in a slip beforehand: fish in batter or stew; rice or pink blancmange? Which combination for Single Room Number Twelve? Straight on to Fourteen, there's no Room Thirteen; nothing for Single Room Number Fourteen.

In a way it's lucky Roland still hasn't got here. If he arrives before Zelda has her first contraction, then she'll be able to say he has seen her all the way through. Roland's her contact, she's so lucky to have him, he can explain, and assuage her fears.

Indeed, as he did when they told her they were going to induce her. Although in principle the Professor made a point of seeing in person any Medical wife at his antenatal clinic, as it happened, he wasn't there that day. A female consultant was there instead of him.

'There!' She patted Zelda's belly. 'We'll have you in on Monday!' She turned away.

'What do you mean?' Zelda struggled to her elbows.

The consultant half-turned. She was tall and broad-shouldered, her hair barbered at the neck, an imitation man. 'We'll have you admitted.'

'No, I mean, what's wrong?' She was panicking. The consultant glanced at her with pity, and then said briskly: 'Nothing wrong. We're just going to induce you, you're lucky. Some are lucky, some are not. You're just one of the lucky ones.'

Her elbows buckled. The consultant's quiffed face looked squarely down. Yes, Zelda was lucky. The wife of a doctor who was going big places. Special personal treatment in one of the top teaching units in the country – not many who had that. And inside knowledge. Luckier than some.

She struggled up again. 'But –'

The consultant had gone.

But Roland sorted it out. Roland talked to Professor, and then explained. He calmed her fears.

Come on, Roland.

That summer she was eight, Zelda wished that someone would explain. There were rumours, the boy brought them, and trailers began to thunder through the village, occasionally slowing, backing up to let each other pass, encroaching on the verges, their steel girders jutting and swinging, giant drums and vast coils of wire making circles of sun. People said someone ought to complain. Hilary had to leave her little brother at home.

What was going on? Mother was vague; Father was always too busy to be bothered, tucked away in the room he used as a study.

She crept in while he was working. He was drawing on the thick wide paper sheets she envied. In all that space you could make a giant coloured pattern, or a picture (if you drew them small) of a hundred people – a whole school, a whole village with a line of different shops, the baker's with brown cobs and orange loaves, the butcher's with meat done in carmine and maroon; and the fishmonger's: what crayon would you use for the fish? Grey was flat, nothing like the silver that fish really were; perhaps green and blue, watery colours, reminding you where the fish had come from?

But Father's drawings were dull. Pale grey lines, very fine and straight, making squares and tubes, and labelled all over with numbers and arrows. No words, nothing labelled with words. 'What's that?' she asked, pointing to a shape larger than the rest, 'that sausage' – though it was really nothing like a sausage, too remote, its lines too straight, its curved end too perfect. 'That's a turbine.' Oh, a turbine, not a sausage. But *turbine*, what was that? The name of the shape, or the name of a thing that the shape represented? She thought: it's better called a sausage. Yet while she thought it, she knew that calling it a sausage didn't make it any easier to understand, or make it seem more real – if anything it made it more unreal than ever.

She said, 'Daddy, can I come on your knee?'

He was surprised, he turned on his chair and looked at her blankly. She felt self-conscious, then quickly scrabbled into the place he'd made by turning. From up on his lap she could see that the drawings made a complicated pattern.

'What are these?' she asked, about a row of circles.

He said in amusement: 'They're the standby pumps.'

His breath had the flat yellow smell of cigarettes.

'And these?' Two little boxes on sticks, like piano keys.

'They're the air pumps.' The tweed of his trousers tickled her leg. She stuck her toe in his turn-up.

'This here,' he said, reaching forward, stroking the lines with his thumb, curling his orange-stained fingers, 'is the transformer, and along here, precipitators.' He leaned further forward; his stomach pressed on her back and his nose poked her head. She could feel him laughing.

'Daddy,' she said, trying to turn and look at his face, 'what was it like where you came from, when you were a little boy?'

He snorted.

She strained round. 'Go on Daddy, what was it like?'

His upper lip curled. His gold filling winked. 'Oh, we were poor. We didn't even have a table.'

'No table?'

'No table.'

'And all those children?'

'Uh-huh.'

'What did you eat off?'

'Well, what d'you think you'd eat off if you had no table? A board on the floor.'

'Go on!'

He sucked something out of his teeth. 'Please yourself.'

'Well, how did you eat off it?'

'How d'you think? We had holes sawn in the floorboards to stick our legs in.'

A plan you could draw with a pencil and compass and ruler: a rectangle bordered by pairs of perfect holes.

'So what did you eat?'

'I told you, we were poor. Mostly nettle stew.'

She stared.

'My mother used to send me and my sisters with buckets to pick nettles, and we filled them up and took them back, and lived off nettle stew.'

'Oh, Patrick, don't tease,' said Mother from the doorway.

Father laughed, a low cackle, and tipped Zelda off his knee. Mother came and stood behind him, and put her hands on his chair. Mother's thumbs moved to and fro on the polished wood behind him. She leaned. 'Don't tease,' she said softly.

Father looked up sharply. 'I'm not teasing,' he snapped, screwing his mouth as though something had stung him. Mother straightened, and stood away.

So it was true, he'd eaten nettles.

There was never the same kind of doubt over what Mother told you. She'd tell you the same thing over and over: 'When I was your age, I didn't spend all my money on sweets. I bought fruit, I'd take sixpence to the shops for a nice juicy pear or a crisp yellow apple. Much better for your health, much better for your teeth, though your grandma would worry so much fruit would give me wind.' Mother acted superbly, hunching her shoulders and reproducing Grandma's low grumble: ' "Watch all that fruit, you'll fart the mattress off the bed!" '

It would take all day to fill buckets with nettles, picking each leaf with care to avoid the acid that lay in wait round its edges. Perhaps they wore gloves. They could pick the tips of the plants, but they'd still have to lean over, brush their arms and bodies on the stinging black bushes.

They thought about it. Hilary picked her nose. Picking your nose a lot, as well as always being hungry, was supposed to be a sign of having worms.

As the foliage thickened, it got darker in the den. A brambly kind of creeper was tangling with the blankets. Inside, they saw each other in a dusky gloom. The little brother didn't come any more, because of the lorries, and also because he always came back crying.

'We're better off without him,' said Annie.

Hilary sighed.

'Here, rock the doll,' said Annie, sneering.

The doll flew; its arms and legs whipped and joggled, and it fell with a thud across Hilary's lap. She sat with her legs splayed, her skirt stretched and riding up to show her white puckery thighs. A strange effect of the light through the blankets showed up their veins as vivid branched deltas. Absently, she stroked the doll's head. Her fingers circled, gently, out of habit, the way they did through her little brother's hair, curling the wisps that had escaped from the plaits.

Annie suddenly shrieked. 'Look what you've *done!*'

Hilary looked down. The doll's hair had come loose. It flapped, above the forehead. She peeled it back. Everyone stared, fascinated. The doll's bald head glimmered. It was pitted all over with rows of holes.

Furiously Annie grabbed the doll back. Then she looked up, her eyes gleaming wickedly. 'Pass me the saucepan.

There, there, did Mummy's baby have a nasty accident?' She slopped her hankie in the saucepan and dabbed the doll's head. 'There, Mummy'll make it better.' The green-brown liquid dribbled through the holes in the skewered head.

'There, she's lovely,' said Annie. 'There, don't laugh.' She folded the hair down again, and laid the doll in her rightful place in the pram, safe from Hilary's hands, to sleep, to be healed by the medicine made out of herbs picked when their power was at its strongest: the optimum moment, hot, full-blown noon.

Seven

SHE DROVE HOME from the antenatal clinic which turned out to be her last. January rain made the streets greasy-black. Five-thirty in the afternoon. Three hours since she drove in the opposite direction. Street lighting shattered in drops on the windscreen, obliterated immediately by the thud of the wipers. She reached the intersection on the south side of the city. Phase traffic lights were in operation, as she approached, they turned to red. She came to a halt.

Traffic sped across in front, along the intersecting road. The red light glowed, haloed through the steam on the windscreen. She wiped the glass with her hand, to widen her view.

Something was wrong. What the female consultant had said didn't make sense.

The lights on the crossroad turned to amber. A taxi which had drawn up beside her on the outer lane nudged forward. She changed into first, ready. The taxi began to roll. Their own amber light came on beneath the red: two haloes, merging. The taxi rolled away. Green. She accelerated and lost her train of thought. Over the crossing the lanes merged and traffic on the right usually tried to nudge in. She concentrated. Cars shuffled in front. She nosed, feeling her way between the pushers and the stragglers. What was it that didn't fit? There was something in the recent past, which if only she recalled it, would throw some light on what the female consultant had said. She groped for the memory, the picture that would satisfy.

The traffic thinned out and became a steady line. Her mind seized on a scene.

There were curtains. And doors.

They called your name.

'Mrs Harris!'

'Oh, it's you!' said the other women, smiling encouragingly, ruefully, enviously, after the delay. 'Your turn.'

Her turn. To jump up, round the corner, and confront a row of doors. Which door? Which is the one she is meant to choose? Not the first, that's engaged, there's the red warning sign which means it's locked; not the next, nor the one after. Is it this one? No: the red warning sign has somehow disappeared, rubbed away; after all it's locked; this is a trick door. It must be the next. No. All the way along, the doors are locked. Oh, but Mrs Harris, you can't go back, wouldn't that look silly, wouldn't that inconvenience everybody – think, you're holding people up, and after there's been so much waiting already: no, you must find the door that is meant for you. She turns in confusion and irritation. A nurse swims up towards her, smiling serenely. 'Here,' she says, helpfully pointing: 'This door, please, Mrs Harris.' This door. Halfway down the row. She pushes it inwards and stands aside so Mrs Harris can enter. So that door was open. Was that a trick door, too?

Inside the door. 'Lock the door, please, after you, Mrs Harris, so the next patient can tell which one is free.' A minute cubicle: a peg for her clothes, a bench for her bottom, a gown hanging on the peg. On the opposite wall not a door, but a curtain, drawn across the view. She undresses, and sits down, hidden behind it. But they know she's there, they haven't forgotten she's waiting to come out, to emerge on the other side when they say the word.

She waits, resting her toes on the cold tiled floor. Every

sound beyond the curtain is clearly audible. She waits, like an actress in the wings ready for her cue, listening while the action plays:

'Mm . . .' This part is the man's. 'I feel the time is ripe.'

Silence. She imagines his hands, scrubbed, well-manicured, moving over the tight shiny mound of a fully pregnant belly. The time is ripe. The huge apple is ripe, the dimple retroverted.

The doctor breaks his silence. 'I should like to bring you in this week.'

'I see.' The woman's voice is calm. It has no note of surprise. She has expected this, she has learned her part well.

Zelda, six months pregnant, the last lap of her pregnancy still before her, waits behind the shutters and pricks up her ears.

'I feel it would be wise.'

What is wrong with the woman? What can be wrong inside the tight skin of her belly?

The woman speaks: 'What day had you in mind?'

'Tomorrow?'

'Ah.' A short pause. 'There's a flower show on tomorrow. I was very much hoping to go.'

'Mm. Well, there's not that much hurry. We wouldn't want you to miss that, not if you've set your heart on it.'

'Mm, rather.'

'Well, go to your flower show. We'll have you in on Monday.'

'Oh, fine. Thank you.'

There's a rustle as the woman's body rouses on the plastic sheet.

'All right?'

'Fine. Thank you.'

The speeches have ended. The Doctor must have gone, exit left. The woman is alone to perform her final actions. Zelda hears her get down from the bed, and then enter the cubicle, alone with her condition. Off to a flower show, with her condition. What condition can it be, that she can take it to a flower show, that it can wait for a flower show? What insidious flaw can grow inside round fruity bellies fast enough to need to be arrested by hospital admission, yet slow enough to wait for a visit to a flower show? The doctor feels it would be wise. What wisdom allows him to distinguish so finely, to know the precise, subtle moment when a visit to a flower show would be no longer safe? As it is, tomorrow the woman will be there, amongst the clotted banks of flowers, plant heads massed and labelled and coded, garnered at the very point when they're most ripely blown.

The flower-show woman rustles, dressing in the next cubicle. Zelda expects her own name to be called.

There is silence beyond the curtain. Everyone seems to have gone away. Have they forgotten her? Have they, after all, forgotten she is waiting in the box with two openings? She went in one end, have they forgotten to get her out the other?

The curtain swishes aside. 'There you are!' A nurse from out of nowhere. Magic. With aplomb, the nurse ushers her out and onto the table where she'll be examined. The nurse checks the notes: twenty-four weeks.

Here comes the Professor. 'Sorry you had such a wait, Mrs Harris.' The explanation for her wait: being seen personally by the Professor.

The Professor says keenly: 'Mrs Harris, would you mind very much if some students come to look at you?'

The students shuffle in.

'How many weeks?' asks the Professor, testing.

A shy student feels.

'Can you tell the fundal height?' asks the Professor, prompting.

Nobody catches Mrs Harris's eye.

The student pokes with his fingers, testing.

'Twenty-four weeks?'

'Very good.'

The Professor catches the nurse's eye.

'Anything else you could comment on?'

The student looks puzzled.

'Well, look at the notes.'

Ah yes. The student nods. Excellent haemoglobin. There is a good rich blood in this patient's veins.

'What about weight?'

The student nods approvingly.

'Test the fat layer.'

The student takes a plastic version of garden shears, and tweaks the skin above her rib cage.

Everyone nods.

The Professor takes her arm and helps her to sit up. He tells the students: 'This is a very healthy patient.' The students cling to his words like whitefly. He takes the skin of her upper arm and rolls it between his finger and thumb. 'This is a very healthy pregnancy.'

Not like the flower-show woman with something insidious that needs careful attention.

This is a very healthy pregnancy.

And this is a very special patient. The Professor gives her a special smile. Thank you Mrs Harris, for letting the students see you. The Professor can count on Mrs Harris to understand. Mrs Harris, above anyone, knows the need for students to get clinical practice. Mrs Harris has the benefit of inside knowledge. And therefore, more than most, the power to help out.

Something still didn't fit. She put her foot down, speeding back from the antenatal clinic that turned out to be her last, eager to talk about it to Roland.

She went up to Roland's study. His door was shut, he was

working – always working, shut away, writing up the research, preparing lectures; most of all, swotting for the Membership exam, that final hurdle, that biggest hurdle, without which all the rest would be in vain, without which he wouldn't, after all, be going big places; the stiffest test after so many years of testing – even the brilliant had been known not to make it and to have to try again; for some it turned out to be their first academic failure: promise dashed, disappointment, ignominy, exposure. It was hard. Sometimes her heart clubbed, seeing him there when she brought him cups of tea: back bent, brow screwed, his curly hair pushed up in twists, wobbly pillars of thumping thick books on the floor all round him. It was awful, she thought, it wasn't fair on him, after all those years of slog, at the age of twenty-eight to be still chained to a desk, and have such a threat hanging over him. But she bit her tongue, resisted the urge to tempt him away, learnt not to mention the theatre, or drinks, disciplined herself not to interrupt, and not to seek his company.

She burst in. She blurted: 'Roland, they're going to induce me!'

She watched him swim up out of his preoccupation, grapple, flounder. He blinked. He couldn't register what she said.

'*Induce?*' He repeated the word.

His face sharpened; he came back up to the everyday world. He turned right round in his chair. 'Induce? Are you sure?'

'Yes, Roland! On Monday!'

He looked at her doubtfully. 'Surely not. You've got it wrong.'

She felt a flick of irritation, and repressed it as quickly – she'd learnt that long ago, not to let her temper loose on Roland; it never worked, it simply drove him back, down under to the slippery private currents of his occupation, from where, grope as she might, she couldn't pull him back to her. And how she needed him now. She said as evenly as her anxiety would let her:

'No, Roland, that's what they said: they're going to induce me on Monday.'

'But *why?*'

'That's just it, Roland, they didn't say. They said there's nothing *wrong*.'

The words hung between them, a puzzle, a jumbled chain, upside down. Inconsistent, not making sense. She flushed. Was it true, she'd got it wrong? She saw herself through Roland's eyes: lay person, out of touch, to whom the words of the priesthood couldn't have any meaning, would only come as an arcane jumble; pregnant woman, blown with hormones that made her flush and cry and jump in fright – a caricature of femininity, too emotionally turbulent to interpret plain English when it hit against her eardrum.

She stood her ground, she squashed that other reality. 'No, Roland, I'm not wrong. It's what they said.'

What, then? She saw a shadow of expression flicker in his eyes. She decided: Worry. Fear. The Chinese puzzle in the air between them seemed to adjust, straighten a little. There must be something wrong. With her body, with their baby. Only, lay person as she was, they hadn't told her, they'd thought they could gloss over the implications of induction. The female consultant had thought it better not to frighten her, not knowing that she was the wife of a doctor, that she had Roland on hand to confirm the inconsistency. So what was wrong?

'Oh, Roland,' she cried, rushing towards him and putting her arms round his shoulders as he sat there. 'Oh, Roland, you can ask the Professor!'

His shoulders were tense, they didn't yield to her pressure. She thought: He's frightened. Her own panic welled.

'You will, won't you?' she said, clinging to his neck, resting her cheek on his woolly head.

'Yes, yes of course,' he said, almost hastily, almost shrugging her off in his effort, she felt, to stop them sinking in panic, to keep them on the course of normality.

She went downstairs, to let him work, and to get the dinner. She picked up a swede, icy-cold, buried all winter and yanked that morning from the hardened soil. She began to peel it. Her knife stuck on a knot, a place where the tense yellow flesh had gone woody.

In an involuntary flash she thought of Roland, riveting himself back to his work and briskly promising.

She was suddenly terribly afraid.

Eight

Lunch time. The bell rings in Single Room Number Fourteen. Staff Nurse goes running. At last, Mrs Harris has had her first contraction. Sister grimaces flirtatiously at Doctor. Has he been wrong then, is it not, after all Primary Inertia? Doctor shrugs, this proves nothing – how do we know it's going to last, this contraction could be merely one of the feeble, widely spaced ones characteristic of the condition. Sister goes off to see.

Mrs Harris lies white-faced, skewed to one side of her bed. She has had a strong contraction, too strong for her first. Better call Doctor.

Doctor comes. 'We'd better turn it down a shade.'

So, not Primary Inertia – interesting try, but he wasn't right this time?

Doctor shrugs again. Well, you can't win them all. Sister must know that, even if he was wrong, it was an enterprising speculation. Sister notices Doctor has very neat ears, laid flat against his head and nestling into his feathery hair.

'Keep an eye on her at the moment,' says Doctor to Sister, and Sister tells Staff Nurse to make sure it's done.

Mrs Harris lies, shattered, and feels her womb begin to gather itself again into a globe of pain.

Since they had completed the spell, they were invulnerable. Or almost: they would have to be careful of counter spells. They would need to take care going past the old woman's cottage. They scrambled out. Long arms of brambles swung over the entrance, spiky and feathery. Now the den was well hidden. While they were gone the doll would be safe inside their magic circle.

They ran down the hill. They had long legs now that bit up the ground; they swallowed the breeze. They crouched and made themselves invisible going past the old woman's cottage. She was out in the garden, her skirt blown like washing, and sure enough, she was calling her pretty little darlings. They kept down and got past. They licked past the unseeing windows of home. No one saw. No one called.

They took the path along the river. Suds of meadowsweet floated in the grass and iris spears came clean out of the water. Further on, said the boy, so his Dad had told him, down near the power station, they had turned the bank into sinking sands. He led the way. His hair stuck up, bristling like wire. He was keen to see, he was keen to show them. 'Come on,' said Annie, hurrying the others. She was keen to keep up, right behind the boy. The sun had come out with a midday pressure.

'My Dad says,' said the boy, 'they could flood the fields if they aren't careful.'

Zelda stopped. She didn't want to go on. Hilary came up short behind her.

Annie hesitated, looking in panic from them to the boy. He was walking away. 'Oh, come on!' Her sparse pigtails trembled.

Zelda stood still. About now at home mother would be out in the garden, bending to pick a lettuce for lunch. The sun would roll across her head as she dipped, and then she'd step back in through the door. The rows of lettuce would be gleaming, green bunches of tissue pushed up through the soil. Inside on the table the potatoes would be cut into chips and heaped in a pile, creamy and wet-looking, beginning to turn orange, cold and powdery and bitter to the tongue. Zelda didn't want to follow.

The boy had slowed to let them catch up. He was punching the surface of the water with stones. Annie twitched with indecision. The boy reached the bend. He gave the briefest look over his shoulder and then turned, out of sight.

'I'm going,' said Annie and began walking off. She broke into a run. Her head and shoulders bobbed, growing smaller, between the banks of wild rhubarb. She had gone.

Hilary and Zelda sat on the bank. A water insect puckered the surface, then disappeared, and left the sheet smooth.

'I'll come back with you,' said Hilary. She put her arm round Zelda's shoulder. She smelt like damp earth. There were fine grey rings in the skin of her neck.

But now, after all, Zelda didn't want to go back. The river stretched ahead, a current of smoothness. They stood up and went on.

They rounded the bend. The field had turned into a sea of mud. Away on the horizon a cloud of white birds rose and fell above a coastline of metal. Toy-truck machines crawled in the distance. The sound of revving came thinly like intermittent radio waves. The wind blew sharply off the edges of the land. Annie and the boy had disappeared.

A high white wall had been slammed up alongside the river. It reared and gleamed. Clouds tumbled across the sky and down behind its rim. From its foot to the water's edge there was eel-grey mud. Abandoned concrete slabs lay strewn across, listing, half-sunk. Sinking sands. The boy had been right. The way was barred.

But they were invulnerable. Nothing could stop them. Zelda stuck out a foot and pressed the nearest slab. It resisted. She brought her whole weight down. The blocks were solid. Where they hadn't sunk, there were magic spots across the sinking sands. They jumped, from one to the other, making their separate jagged routes across the shiny expanse.

After a while, they stopped and looked round. They had come a long way. The wall reared on one side, sheer and bright. On the other, the river welled as black as oil. Was the sun out, or had it gone in? Zelda looked back at Hilary, whose wobbly-toy figure swayed and then righted. Hilary shouted, her voice came out, jumped away from her body, and shrivelled in the air. The wind sliced along the wall.

'Hey!'

Another voice.

It came from above. They looked up.

Over the top of the wall the head and shoulders of a policeman were jutting.

He called again. The sound was thin, far away. He jerked his arm, and metal bits winked on his hat and shoulders.

'Come off there –' His voice flew up and dropped away. He waved, he couldn't get them, a black shape against a wide-open sky, a Punch-and-Judy policeman.

The slab Zelda was standing on squelched beneath her like a spoon in jelly. It was standing still that was dangerous; you must jump, keep going, not heed any warning. They went on leaping. When they next looked, the policeman had gone: an empty blank where he'd been; only the clouds still tumbling, sucked in beyond the rim. As though he'd never been there.

And so they kept going, and got to where there was a gap in the wall. They stopped and stared through wire netting. The power-station site. On the flattened, pinched land lorries shunted and tipped and workmen moved like insects. Building sheds squatted, higgledy-piggledy, among raw piles of gravel. Beyond it all, against the sky, gleamed four huge constructions, white and circular, the beginnings of four gigantic cauldrons.

Going back they caught sight of Annie and the boy again, two bright beads bobbing way out on the muddy field.

They set out to catch them. Now no one could stop them, they could defy anyone; from a trench in the distance, over the horizon, down over the other side of the world, the luminous orange shoulders of workmen poking up seemed only like glove puppets. The earth stood in ridges and troughs marked with deep patterns from caterpillar wheels. It was soft; they teetered and sank; it came over their ankles and marked their socks red. Their feet sucked and sprang, leaving prints so deep the shape wasn't clear, disturbing thick black puddles streaked with rainbow colours.

A sound cracked the air. They looked up, losing balance. The mud collapsed as they wobbled; they sawed the air with their arms. And then it was above them: the huge back of a lorry, jutting metal and caked earth, coming at them. They scrabbled. The lorry steered towards them. The engine roared, blotting up everything. A mud wave dipped: Zelda fell.

The wheels stuck; they spun; the engine screamed. The gob of her own scream leapt up and was lost. The jagged rubber bit, and rolled once more towards her.

All at once she was weightless; her body followed her arms, she slipped, shot through the mud. She lay still, face down.

Hilary let go, released her clamp round Zelda's wrists. Zelda climbed to her knees. The lorry had passed, over the place where she had fallen, and round in an arc. It stopped, the engine running, the frame shuddering. They stared. The cab was empty. No driver.

Someone in the cab sat up, there was a driver after all. His huge eyes popped; he couldn't believe them. He raised his fist and swore out of the window, but as he brought the lorry forward again, he simply stared, bull-necked and craning sideways. How could they be there, when before he hadn't seen them? Were they really there now? They had been invisible. All too visible now, they took to their heels, escaped across the field and caught Annie and the boy up on the road. The others shrieked with luscious fear and admiration.

'Cor, what have you been doing?'

Zelda looked down her front. She was covered from chest to feet with mud, she was a walking wall of mud.

They set off towards home. The road was quiet, but at any moment a lorry could thunder round the next bend. They listened out. Bees hummed in the verges. From somewhere ahead came a rhythmic tock and a puckered echo. They came round the bend and saw a man driving a post into the side of the road. His sleeves were rolled, his piston forearms punched. His jacket, slung on the fence, bore the letters of the electricity board. He stopped as they approached and leaned on his post. He pushed his cap back off his forehead and bright yellow hair bristled up.

They slowed, in a gang, and stared back as they passed. He screwed his eyes. What could he see? Could he see them as they saw each other: Zelda behind her hardening wall, Annie with her shining aerial plaits, Hilary buried in her fatness, and the boy all tight inside his dry mottled skin?

He squinted uncertainly. He drew his lips back with the difficulty, showing blue-white teeth. Then he turned away and began driving his post again. A dark stain, like oil or blood, blotted the shirt between his shoulder blades.

They went on. At the next bend, Zelda turned. The man was standing still again. He was looking intently down the road to the place where they were.

They noticed the briars had hard green flower buds. With frilly feelers, like camouflaged insects. Wild rose buds.

Something stank in the den. What was it? A dead rat? Had somebody left some half-eaten food? A wet-dustbin smell, a smell of rotten cabbage. They turned things over. The smell was in the pram.

They lifted the doll and brown liquid dripped from the joint in her neck. Her body came upright and a pivot in her head moved her eyes open. Annie jabbed them shut with two fingers, this wasn't the moment for her to waken. The spell had gone wrong. The medicine had rotted. They tipped her up. Brown liquid oozed from the holes in her head.

They stiffened. They'd all heard it, the tell-tale sound; twigs snapping. But when they looked out there was no one to be seen.

They would have to be careful. You always had to be careful. Even the fishes promised nothing for ever. Plop. Oh, Queen, thy wish shall be granted, thou shalt have a child. A bubble of life from the bottom of the river. But that didn't stop the thirteenth fairy, the witch, creeping up with a different promise.

Nine

IN THE LAST stages of her pregnancy, she lost her touch with cooking. The stew with swede wasn't tasty. Still, they ate it. It was a dark winter's evening. She switched on the lamp and laid the table. Outside in the garden bare trees swayed, and behind them suburban street lamps trembled. The wind warped the telegraph wires. She drew the curtains. The lamp glowed, round as the swede, and cast a pool along the wall.

The stew was ready. She called Roland from his study. He came into the room. His shirt collar shone in the light from the lamp. They sat, one each side of the table, and began to eat.

'You will do it, won't you?' she said.

He looked up, his spoon poised. After a moment, he said, 'What?'

'You'll speak to the Professor?'

'Yes.' His shoulders hunched. She was filled with fear. What was he thinking? What was it he wasn't voicing?

'What's wrong, Roland?'

'Nothing. Nothing.' He put his spoon down. He looked at her then, over his glasses, his eyes intent, two dark marbles. 'Look, Zelda. You mustn't worry. I'm perfectly sure you've nothing to worry about. McGuirk is the topmost specialist in his field. In the world. I think we can trust him.'

'Trust him?' Over *what* did they need to trust him? What could it be that was wrong?

Roland turned to his plate. His forehead shone at her, hard and compact. He said intently, 'We can trust him, Zelda, to provide the best medical care available.'

She sat, nursing the implications. *Medical*: Illness.

'Look, Zelda. If he says you've got to go in now and be induced, you can be sure there must be a very good reason.'

Now panic.

He was eating his stew again.

'But then, what *is* it, Roland, what can be wrong?

She thought: He knows, but, like them, he won't say.

He looked up in surprise. 'Why, nothing, necessarily.'

She was shocked. At his surprise. Had she been getting him wrong, did he not, after all, see any inconsistency? If not, what – what was going on?

'Zelda, nothing *probably*. Most probably it's just a precaution.'

'Against *what?*'

He jerked his hand across the table, caught hers brusquely. '*Anything*, probably. You're just being given extra special care. Because of me, don't you see?' He smiled at her ruefully. Her heart pinched itself quickly: for a moment, she had failed to trust him. Yet she was lost, still she didn't understand. She tried to search his eyes for the explanation, but he dropped them quickly. And when he raised them again she could see they were frightened. She thought: He's lost as well, he also doesn't understand. She thought: We're in it together.

She took her hand out from under his and placed it on top, and stroked his knotted knuckles. 'Well,' she said, encouragingly, consolingly, 'maybe, after all, there has been a misunderstanding. If there's nothing wrong, then perhaps I won't have to – oh, God, honestly, Roland, I *really* don't *want* to. You will talk to the Professor?'

'Yes,' he said, and he seemed to cheer up. 'I'll get his reassurance.'

A piece of undercooked carrot caught in her throat. She coughed it up, choking over her own poor cooking.

She said, 'I'm sorry about the stew.'

He laughed. He seemed relieved. He said, 'What did you do wrong?'

'I can't tell, can you?'

'Too little salt?'

She shook her head, she thought most likely she'd been wrong with her timing – also, there was something lacking in the swede, perhaps it was too old, perhaps it had been locked by frost in the earth too long. They scraped their plates in silence. She felt deflated, not relieved. Suspicion winked again. Was he telling the truth? Surely, whizz-kid that he was, he'd know something she didn't, some medical fact, some obstetric possibility?

'I don't understand, Roland, why you've so little idea yourself what might be the reason.'

He said quickly: 'It's not my area. You know very well that General Medicine doesn't cover Obstetrics. And I've been so busy with the specialist research, I've been getting out of touch . . . There's just no time . . . I must find more time to keep up with the journals . . .' His glasses flashed wild signals. 'After all, I need to keep up, for the Membership exam . . .'

'Have more stew,' she said in desperation.

Outside the wind was getting stronger, blowing distorted sounds through the telegraph wires. Their shadows loomed on the wall in the circle of lamplight; one straight and thin, the other curved and fat. Jack Sprat and his wife.

The student nurse peers with alarm. 'Are you all right, Mrs Harris?'

Mrs Harris has her eyes closed. Her arms are splayed, hanging loosely over the side of the bed.

'All right, Mrs Harris?'

Mrs Harris fails to respond. She's breathing deeply. Is she asleep? Is she unconscious? At last her breathing subsides, and she moves her hands, composes them back on her belly, and opens her eyes.

'Yes, thank you,' she says, from a very long distance.

Mrs Harris was doing her relaxation. Mrs Harris has learnt how to ride with the pain.

'Oh, very good, Mrs Harris,' says Staff Nurse, coming in at that moment. 'Very good, well done.'

Sister tells Doctor: 'Mrs Harris's contractions are still very strong.'

'How many's she had now?'

'Three in ten minutes.'

'They should lessen quite soon now the dosage is turned down.'

Sister is satisfied.

'Doctor . . .' she calls.

Doctor turns. His white coat swings. His neat ankle swivels. He raises a black eyebrow. The corners of his mouth twitch. 'Andrew,' he says.

'Oh, *Andrew*,' says Sister. Sister pauses. Sister's aware the expression on her face gives her high cheekbones. 'Could you sign these?'

'Sure,' says Andrew, and takes them and signs with a flourish. Not every houseman is as co-operative as Andrew.

'Have you eaten yet, Andrew?'

Andrew grimaces. Of course he's not eaten. Andrew the houseman doesn't get time.

'I'll make you tea and biscuits, come into my office.'

Ten

'What are you thinking there?'

Zelda opens her eyes.

The West-Indian nurse is back. How they come and go, changing and chopping, floating away and flickering back. Dark butterflies, pale moths.

'Talking in your sleep! What's on your mind?' She leans over and touches Zelda's brow. Her large bosom dips and brushes the air with a faint sweet smell.

She says: 'You look done in. I think you could do with something to buck you up, hey?' She smiles like a film star. 'Are you thinking about your little baby? He won't be long now.'

Zelda stares in amazement.

No, Zelda is not thinking about her little baby.

No, she is having no maternal feelings.

The nurse looks concerned. 'Oh, honey!' she exclaims. 'Don't you worry, now, everything's fine! He'll come much quicker this way.' She touches the drip; gestures towards the electrodes.

'Your husband come?'

Zelda looks up sharply. She doesn't know. Did he? How long has she been asleep? What's the time? Cluck. The clock on the wall says, 'Three.'

Three o'clock. Things are slack. Andrew has more tea in Sister's office. She fills his cup. 'Thanks, Barbara,' he says.

Barbara smiles. Her cheekbones are higher than ever, lifted without conscious effort, entirely automatic, not aching in the least.

Staff Nurse comes to report. 'Excuse me, Sister.' She knocks on the door. She rolls her big eyes and smiles her glossy smile. Sister stares, slightly hostile. Why did she knock? What was she implying?

Andrew smirks and takes his foot off the table.

'Excuse me Sister, I think Mrs Harris has gone out of labour.'

Andrew answers, quick as a flash: 'Thank you Nurse, I'll be along.'

'You think we can give her something to keep her strength up, Sister? She seems very weak.'

'All right,' says Andrew, 'We'll see to it.'

Staff Nurse grins and floats away.

'Damn,' says Andrew, 'she's bloody difficult, this one.'

Sister looks up. This one, the staff nurse? Has he noticed her insolence? Oh, Sister sees: Mrs Harris.

He sucks air through his teeth. 'Hm.' He taps his fingers on the table. 'Secondary Inertia.'

Barbara arches her feet so her ankles look slimmer. 'It's a blessing, isn't it,' Andrew says dreamily, moving his own feet a fraction towards them, 'that in cases like this, where there's so little happening, the machine can take over the observing and measuring, leaving staff free for other things . . .'

Three o'clock. Halfway through the two-hour antenatal clinical. The Senior Lecturer hands Arleen Manning the foetal stethoscope. Arleen approaches the huge belly on the bed. She places the metal ring on the brown stretched skin. A small gasp is emitted from the woman's face down beyond the sheets, and the belly wobbles. Arleen waits while it subsides. She listens, and counts. She pronounces decisively, 'A hundred and forty beats to the minute.'

He raises an eyebrow.

'Normal,' she adds, with a hint of contempt. The first secret in teaching: assess the level of those you try to teach. Arleen knows that, while still a student, well before she gets to be a teacher.

Everyone crowds back through the curtain. The Senior Lecturer remains to speak to the patient, so the students are left on their own for a moment. Rick Jenkins nudges up to Arleen.

'Did you finish those notes?'

She doesn't answer, she waits for him to go on. He hesitates, and blushes. 'Are you able to lend them?'

'No,' she says shortly, 'I didn't get round to it, and I'm afraid they're indecipherable.' She gives him a steady look with her head slightly bent, the look he identifies with women in authority, women teachers, women lawyers, career women, his mother. She says: 'It's in the textbook, of course.'

'Yes,' he says, 'yes, of course.'

Arleen thinks back to the part of the lecture where Rick Jenkins got lost. It's clear in her head: the ray of sun has moved across and down and falls on the desk, lighting up the Professor's hands, spread like stars as he bends and sums up:

'The foetal monitor we have now is one of the greatest steps forward in obstetric technology. By continuous monitoring of the uterine contractions and of the foetal heart sounds, it may be possible to obtain advance warning of foetal distress – which, as we have seen' (he waves behind him) 'can result in permanent damage or death to the foetus.

'We must always bear in mind that the foetus has been aptly called the hidden patient. It has not been easy until now to discover when and to what extent the foetus is suffering from lack of oxygen. The latest monitor helps us to guard against this danger and so to know more precisely the point at which it may be necessary to assist delivery surgically.'

He raises his hands to signal the end and for one second, as they flick out of the light and join the rest of him in the shadow – his blue suit, his tufted head, all the bits coming together – he looks like a scarecrow.

Arleen smiles inwardly. There are little holes in the myth of his charisma. Not everyone sees them. Arleen can see them. With her special powers. She is better than any of them. These are the days of opportunities for women. She'll be better than any of them, mere men, pretend gods, who have gone before her.

The witch had been there in their absence. They could tell by the sign. A dead bird on the leaves, wings swastika-hooked, the head all but ripped from the body, hanging by a thread. The speckled breast was matted with blood, dusty, bitty, hardly distinct from the leaves and stones. Should they bury it? No, it was a trick. They mustn't touch. They would have to leave it, skirt round it, slew their eyes sideways each time to remind themselves of the constant danger.

Where did the souls of birds go when they died? Better not ask. Better not think of it.

She opens her eyes. The room seems white. What has happened to the light? Someone's feeling her pulse. Something flutters on her belly, butterflies, insects, jumping, tickling: her gown being lifted. Someone's head bends above her belly, the back of a head, black waves lying close, in one place an ear sprouting like a shoot from a potato. The head lifts, recedes, a voice comes out of it, on the other side of it, directed away to the wall of the room.

'Everything's OK. She's just become a little weak. You're right, she'd better have something.'

What will they bring her? The sounds recede. Oh honey, said the staff nurse with the bosom like melons, Oh honey what can I bring you, melon swimming in honey and Jamaican rum?

The nurse appears at the bedside. What's she carrying? Another bottle. A different solution. She unclips the first bottle, snaps the second in its place. 'There, this will make you feel better.' The liquid shakes and glitters, sends out rays, a small star exploding. On the opposite wall its refracted image shoots and flickers: northern lights, signs on the sky.

How did she do that? How was it possible? How can you stop the flow to change the bottle, without making an air lock? What if she's made one and hasn't noticed? What if a bubble of air is travelling now down the tube towards her vein? It could give her an embolus. A bubble of air stopping life like a pebble.

'Nurse,' she calls weakly, but the nurse is gone.

The boy touched the bird. That was what did it. He kicked it into the bushes, and it stuck there, swinging. And then angry life welled up out of its feathers: green and blue flies welling up and shooting off at tangents into the air. Then he tried to bury it, kicked dead leaves roughly over it, but the life kept oozing, iridescent bubbles still escaping from under the leaves.

A wind rustled the branches. The wood had gone dark.

'I'm going home,' said Zelda, and no one protested.

They straggled away to their various homes.

She came in through the gate. A black shape was poised on the roof. The bird had got there before her. Perched on a ridge tile, it saw her coming. She must get round the corner of the house to the door. It knew that. Comically, a mechanical bird, making fun of her, it shuffled, jerked, along the line of the roof, one foot after the other, until it reached the gable end. It leaned over and looked down.

She dared not move. She was trapped. She couldn't get past. It scissored its beak wide, snap-snap, laughing into the air. Its bullet head turned, its steely eye cocked: Come on. I dare you, come on, try getting past me! The sun came out through a gap in the clouds, briefly, a yellow sheet flapping. In that moment she could see she was right, she wasn't mistaken, she could see the bird for what it was: its breast lit up with iridescent colours, the fluorescent light of underworld.

Eleven

CHRISTMAS. EIGHT MONTHS into her pregnancy. Roland warns: 'Zelda, don't eat too much Christmas cake. Or Christmas pudding, or mince pies.' Roland can tell her that animal fats, and sugar, and purified starch are bad for her body, for anyone's body, they can thicken the arteries and slow down the blood. And if they're bad for the mother, they can't be good for the foetus. And she must think of the baby. Baby first. She must eat the right things. And eat in moderation. A fat pregnant woman will have a fat baby. Fat babies aren't healthy.

Zelda's stomach rumbled.

Though after that, anyway, towards the end, she lost her appetite.

She heard the gate bang in the garden. She flipped the blind up and looked out. Was it Roland? She couldn't tell. Maybe the wind getting up again. There it was now in the trees, scraping the swing in the next-door garden, blowing through the keyhole, scrabbling like rats at the lock. The key turned quarter-circle. Roland pushed the door in.

The wind had tufted his hair, it stood on end, bent over the wrong way. He got inside, out of the gusts, and flattened it down, which for some reason made her feel better.

'Did you speak to the Professor?' He hadn't got his coat off, he hadn't even put his case down. His face was reddened from the wind – a few steps through the elements between the car door and the house and he was ruffled all over, bemused and goggled, his glasses steamed with the transition indoors.

'Yes.' He dropped his case. His face jerked down and away and then back up again, an off-on beacon. Tense. She held her breath, antennae out to assess the cause of it. Bad news?

The pause lengthened. He didn't go on. Was he dismayed? Irritated? Yes, that was it. She had blundered. She had bullied, challenged. Again, she'd shown no faith. Of course he'd seen the Professor. And now she had spoilt things, implying he might not have, implying criticism. And now he'd be on edge, there'd be too many tensions, too many undercurrents, for him to talk unhindered, and let her see for herself the whole truth, the essence, of his conversation with the Professor.

'What did he say?' Part of her stood back and watched herself nagging, insistent, face thrust forward towards him still struggling out of his coat. But she'd waited so long: all day inside the house, watching the telegraph wires turn from morning silver to afternoon red, at length to black against a cold greenish sky. She thought he might have rung. All day she'd kept stopping when out of immediate earshot, imagining, listening for the bell.

Roland stood half out of his coat, one empty arm flapping. 'It's OK. There's nothing wrong. It's just a precaution.'

What to feel? Relief? Yes, relief: that's what she should feel. Nothing wrong. She waited for the feeling of relief to flood her. It didn't come. Why not? Because she'd bungled. She'd set up tensions, and so she had distorted Roland's behaviour. She had made him guarded, and so she couldn't trust the spontaneity of his account.

He was moving forward, about to pass her; then he was level, and after that he was past, making through the hall. Had he no more to say, had he really no more to say to her? She put out a hand.

'Roland! Precaution? Against what?'

He came back. He lifted two palms. 'I don't know . . . anything. Any of the complications of late pregnancy. They're just making absolutely sure that everything goes properly.'

Yes, that would be right: a doctor's wife, they would want to make sure of things. Then the fist of anxiety inside her clenched tighter: 'What precisely did he say?'

Roland's lips made a hyphen. She panicked. She was doing it again, testing him out, calling him to account like a schoolmarm. Failing to trust. She mustn't quiz him. She mustn't get his back up, otherwise so many things got in the way.

'Just that. That he thinks it's a good idea if you come in on Monday to make absolutely sure that everything goes properly.' His voice was choked as a parrot's.

The panic grew. She wasn't getting to the bottom of it, Roland was itching to be off, into the kitchen.

'Roland, precisely what did you ask him?'

His jaw worked subtly. He was gritting his teeth. 'I asked him, just as I said I would, why it was necessary for you to go in on Monday.'

Zelda put her hands behind her, and caught the coats hanging on the wall, husks, hanging limp, with a wintery cold feel to the fabric. She leaned back, and they sank inwards, and her elbows hit the wall. Outside the wind made tunnels of the emptiness of the telegraph wires. That wasn't what she'd wanted: for him to ask why it was necessary. No, not to ask why. She had wanted him to find out if it was necessary at all.

He had failed her. To assume it was necessary. Not to challenge. How precisely must he have put it? Professor, could I have a word with you, I'm rather concerned . . . ? Professor, I'd be glad if you'd set my mind at rest . . . ? Look here, old chap . . . no, not that one, Lecturers don't speak to Professors of Medicine like that. More likely Sir, . . . She sighed. Of course it would be Sir. Of course it would be why. Not if. And under what circumstances had he asked the question? Had he gone to his room, knocked on the door, made a special visit and so underlined his concern and the importance of his question, gained the Professor's undivided attention?

'Where did you see him?' She couldn't help it.

His jaw puppet-jerked under the stress of her cross-examination. 'I went up to the ward. I knew I'd catch him there. He's a very difficult man to catch, you know.'

He came towards her, he was drained. Oh, that was true, she could imagine that. After all, Roland had done well. He might easily not have caught him at all. But he did: using his initiative, and going out of his way, to catch the Professor on his ward. And the Professor would look up, and come away when he could, and give him a moment, and explain everything quickly and efficiently. Explain why. Not if.

'Oh, Roland.' She reached out and held his hands. He had small hands for a man. She had large hands for a woman. They could swap and borrow gloves: they had hands the same size. Roland knew at the start he would never make an obstetrician; his hands were too small, his fingers too short. He turned to other areas, he concentrated on research.

She held his small hands. 'Roland, come and lie down.'

He lay against her, his purple penis immediately erect. No sex. They couldn't. It hurt her now. If only they could: she touched his arms. They were rigid, muscles clenched. He gazed at the ceiling. Already his erection was fading. The brief idea, the memory, had excited his body, and then had slipped off like a fish into underwater weeds. He was a long way away.

'What's wrong?'

'I'm so bloody tired.'

He turned his head her way, but his eyes, unseeing, marked out his problems. 'I've got so much on. The research, the exam, the clinical work, and on top of it all the teaching . . .'

And he had made time to see the Professor. And instead of showing appreciation she had demanded, and nagged.

He said, 'I've got a bloody lecture now to prepare for tomorrow.'

Her heart sank. In the frame of mind he was in, he would worry about that. Tease it, fret about it, and be up all hours. She didn't understand it: why would he suddenly, occasionally, plunge into despondency, some kind of crisis of confidence? He'd always done so well. He had the best qualifications, the best junior jobs, the best references. Of course, there was the Membership threat; if asked, he'd say it was that that was getting him down – but she knew it wasn't just that, it had always been like this; when things were fine, going well, he'd suddenly flounder, seem almost desperate. And she couldn't stand it, it frightened her: why? She would wait, frightened sick, for the crisis to pass. And it always did. When did he ever make a mess of a lecture or write a rotten paper? But somehow that knowledge couldn't comfort. When the crisis was on she would freeze up tight inside her own dead panic. Why? she asked herself, flailing around for answers: was she so incapable of sympathy, or of helping – was she so dependent on his being strong? But of course, after all she knew what it was: every so often the knowledge surfaced. It did now: the crisis was her fault; if he couldn't cope tonight, it was because she'd upset him.

She drew a finger up to his shoulder. 'You'll be all right.'

He turned his head away, transferred the map of his problems to the opposite wall. She looked up the line of his neck and round the bowl of his head. His hair, straightened now, brushed back from his forehead, followed the curve and flicked to a down-curled tail at the nape. She liked that: it was sleek, feathery, growing the shape that his head had grown. The image popped up of his hair on end earlier, floating, like something fake coming off. She squashed the image quickly.

Why, not if. She said suddenly: 'But Roland, why induce me? A week before term? Roland,' she pulled herself up, hands flat on his chest, 'there must be something wrong!'

He sat up then and put his arms about her. 'There's nothing wrong, Zelda. Nothing at all. He said everything's perfect. He says you're a very healthy pregnancy. He's very pleased with your progress.'

She looked up for the truth of it, stared him in the eyes. He took a breath. Something else was coming.

'He did say there was just one very minor thing that might or might no indicate problems . . .'

For God's sake. 'What's that?'

'He says you've stopped gaining weight. That could be an indication that the placenta is beginning to deteriorate.'

'Why didn't you tell me?'

He grabbed her as she flung herself out. 'I didn't want to panic you. It doesn't necessarily meant that that's happening. They just want to be sure.'

Ill, or not? Complications, or not? She couldn't cope.

Her will clubbed: 'No. No, I won't. I won't be induced.'

He held her wrists. He held tight. His hands were only the same size as hers, she could wrench free with an effort. He held on, he was hurting. He seemed desperate to persuade her. She thought wildly: *He* can't cope, the situation *must* be desperate, it must be imperative. He went on in a voice that was almost vicious: 'Zelda, *think!* Just think about it! Do you think he wouldn't tell *me* his honest opinion? We have to trust his judgement. In view of who we are, he's bound to be especially careful, for our sakes – and for his own. For his own reputation. Come on, Zelda, calm down.'

He bent his head to her shoulder and his neck-feathers shifted. He kissed her shoulder, her neck, finally her mouth. His lips were soft. His knotted penis rose, huge, far too large for her crammed, oppressed body.

He murmured: 'Zelda, you have to think about the baby. We have to do what is best.' He drew back and said intently: 'Mothers don't die nowadays in childbirth. Babies still do. It's the baby we must think of. We must do whatever is advised to ensure the baby's safety.'

Oh, yes, he was right. He was so right. Baby first. Oh, God, she must call on her dried-up selfish soul.

'Don't cry,' he said, scooping the tears from her cheeks with his soft nibbling lips, 'don't cry, sweetheart, don't cry,' nuzzling, licking, scooping up her panic, on top of everything else, all his other problems, taking it from her, taking it over. He had tried to protect her, he had been prepared to shoulder alone the burden of worry. On top of everything else. She stroked his back, faintly damp and warm with his own particular greasiness. She clung to him. He was all she had, she was alone but for him in this alien place, this city knotted with concrete and ribbed with wires.

It was this, after all, that would be the truly strong thing: to control her instinct to fight; to give in, acquiesce, for the sake of something other than herself.

Twelve

IT WAS A technique, to be learned. Like an ancient art, something like yoga. Although they claimed this was new, lately developed, until very recently taught in only the most progressive hospitals, still not available everywhere, so you were lucky to have it. And you'd a duty to take advantage of it; if you didn't there'd be no excuse, no cause for complaint on the day.

Now, on the day, four o'clock in the afternoon, at long last they have Zelda's contractions under control. Occurring at ten-minute intervals, each lasting for forty seconds, they make a satisfactory pattern, normal, acceptable, for halfway through the first stage of labour. A roll of graph paper records them, a clean tongue protruding out of the machine.

Zelda practises the technique. She is in control. A voice-over guides her, the disembodied voice that flitted, sideways and back again, resting, rising up again, down beyond the rows of bellies. Vinyl tiles and rubber mats, sun falling in strips and warming those who lay in its path. 'Have a rest, ladies, relax, drift off to sleep.'

Go to sleep, children. Floorboards and rubber mats. Boxes of light that had dropped in through the window, and those children they'd trapped lit up startlingly, their skin so pale it was bluish, hair turned bright yellow or red, their whole bodies glowing, but so separate, so transformed, they seemed almost dead. And if you were trapped in one yourself, you throbbed, getting drowsy, seeing nothing beyond wriggling darkness.

Zelda lies on the bed, drowsy between contractions. Time flows, circular, like blood. Progress isn't linear.

But they are looking at the clocks.

Four-thirty. They are looking at their watches, breast-watches, upside-down watches, on a doctor's hairy wrist a digital watch glowing with phosphorescent light, bristling with push-buttons, flicking the single seconds into unrelated, temporary existence and then away into oblivion. They are measuring. Measuring her pulse, the rate her blood is flowing through her body. The machine is measuring, measuring the contractions, the rate at which her womb gathers itself up, gradually retracts, the muscle thickening at one end like the crown of a turnip. And measuring the foetal heart rate, tracing the pulse that throbs along the foetal skull, recording how it changes, slows, for half a minute at a time, as the muscle contraction compresses the blood vessels that run to the placenta.

And Zelda drifts, drops her fingers, lets the tension float from the ends of them, and rides with the pain.

But now she needs to turn on her side. No longer can she cope with the pain lying flat on her back. The pain bears down on her, grinding her body beneath it. She must turn, curl round it to contain it, trap it round with the rest of her body. She swings her left arm to turn. The drip stand rattles. It seems to wobble; she flinches. The strap strains round her belly.

Now she lies slewed, her arm painfully behind her. Her belly is suspended, not resting on the sheet, not cradled, but a full bag hanging, crammed with foetus and placenta, inadequate placenta, a sponge squeezed of goodness, pale, emptied of red blood, unable to nourish. Bad veins, bad placenta, inadequate mother who must be strapped to a machine.

But that doesn't fit. A shutter clicks in her head. All along they have congratulated her on her health. A very healthy pregnancy. Excellent haemoglobin, an almost perfect curve on the weight chart. Nothing wrong with the blood, under the skin a perfect layer of fat. Healthy eater with a healthy body. Maybe eating a little too much on occasion, Christmas for instance: nothing to do but eat two big meals a day, in spite of Roland's warnings; the whole world closed in to firelight and holly and fattening food. And she, unlike others, unable to walk it all off with three bracing miles through the frozen semi-country – spaces rigid with pylons, garbage petrified in the canal; no, round and slow, she must stay at home. But she made up for it afterwards, listening to Roland, she ate less, cut down – after that, anyway, losing her appetite.

She stops breathing. That's it. That explains the levelling in her weight. She got too fat, and she deliberately slimmed again. She distorted the chart. And on the strength of that they decided her placenta might be failing. They looked at a figure on a chart. They asked her no questions, nothing about her life or her eating habits that could give the figure another meaning. They made an arbitrary decision.

They decided to do this to her. Lay her out and strap her up and pump a synthetic drug into her blood. And maybe air. They could kill her. She turns back, strains, letting out her breath again, to look at the tube leading from the bottle. Are those bubbles? Her breath comes quickly, panic breaths, at the same time another contractions begins, and she isn't ready, she isn't in control. The contraction seizes her, a giant hand descending and grabbing round the middle and crushing the life out; she's like a rubber doll, helpless. But oh, she can feel, she can hear: faraway, muffled, another voice-over.

'Mrs Harris! What's this? Good gracious me, you'll scare the other patients!'

She is screaming. She stops. The sound cuts, like a radio turned off. Her breath comes in quick sharp bits. The contraction is fading.

The nurse says, 'Now come on. You were doing so well. Remember your exercises, you haven't forgotten them, have you?' She shoots a meaningful glance. 'And think about your baby. You haven't forgotten him, have you? He's best if you're calm. That's a good girl.'

There's a pause. The nurse says with a new tone, 'Are they getting too much? Would you like an injection?'

'No!' Zelda pulls herself up.

The nurse pushes her back. 'You must relax, Mrs Harris! Now get yourself comfortable. Try not to panic. Are you sure you wouldn't like an injection for the pain?'

No. That's the last thing, that's the main thing. She must keep alert. She must tell Roland what she's realised, she must be awake to tell him when he comes. Where is he? Has he really not come, after all this time – has he come, and she been sleeping? You have to keep on guard or dreadful things happen.

Afterwards no one kept guard in the woods. They'd lost interest, they'd got scared. The doll was left to rot. Only the bird in the bush kept sentry, beaked skull, witch's token, hanging on the branches where the boy had kicked it, birdbones left by a darkly flitting soul. And when they went back, Hilary and Zelda, they were frightened. They held hands and crept up. For a moment, they were confused, they didn't recognise the place. They stood amazed: the den had become a bank of wild roses. Butterflies dropped and rose on the blossom. They exclaimed, and ran forward, their fear subsiding. They were unprepared for the horror that lay inside.

'Mrs Harris, here's the Professor to see you.'

Five o'clock. The Professor's calling in on his way home. But where's Roland, the Professor will be gone for good when he comes now, when she tells him the trick she thinks they have played on her. She must confront the Professor. She must tell him she knows.

But it's too late. Now it's done. Telling won't mend things. And it will be impossible to tell him. She knows that, the minute he comes to her bedside: he's so white, his coat shining, no other hospital laundry has this glow, and the lines of it so straight, so perfectly pressed, his skin is a different pink from other people's flesh, like meat under special lighting in a butcher's window – he's a different creature, not a creature you could talk to.

She tries. 'Professor, the other day, when my husband came to talk to you . . .'

He smiles politely, quizzically.

'About my being induced . . .'

His eyes flick up to the ceiling, trying to place the occasion. He can't remember, his eyes roll, cogs turn inside, pictures shutter: this moment, that – when, what occasion was this, what conversation? And then, jackpot, he has it, his eyes light up, two black bunches of grapes.

'Oh, yes, Mrs Harris, that's right, you were worried, weren't you? Well, as I explained to your husband, there's absolutely nothing to worry about. This is something we have begun to do all the time now. It's much safer, we have found, for both the mother and baby.'

He smiles, waiting for her to register, and show him her pleasure.

'But no . . . he said . . . you said . . . about the placenta . . .'

He looks confused, and then memory triggers: 'Oh, yes, that's right, your weight had flattened, hadn't it? Well, that is of course an additional indication . . .'

An additional indication. Not the main one after all for

bringing her here and doing all this. The main one something else: a matter of habit, a matter of general safety . . . But no, that can't be right, there's something that makes it surely a matter of emergency.

'But not yet term . . . only thirty-nine weeks . . .'

He answers pat: 'Oh, that's optimum time, we've found, for routine induction.'

She opens her mouth. He adjusts, his face sets.

'We would, of course, in any case, have had to take measures, in view of your failure to continue to gain weight. We have to put first and foremost any risk to the baby . . .'

Her womb clenches. She closes her eyes. The spasm wells, and subsides. When she opens her eyes the Professor is gone.

They would have done it anyway. They have specially chosen her, because she's so healthy. At thirty-nine weeks, when, in their opinion, the placenta is long past its maximum efficiency.

She ought to have known, she read the textbook, she should have read between the lines, guessed the implications. She nagged Roland, and eventually he brought it, an obstetric textbook from the Medical Library. He brought it dubiously, under pressure. She shouldn't be reading it. She'd see things that would worry her. She'd make wrong connections, and frighten herself silly. A little knowledge is a dangerous thing.

She read it there in black and white, the night before she was due to come into hospital: *Any condition may be an indication for induction if it is considered safer for the mother, or for the foetus, or for both, that the pregnancy does not continue any longer.*

Any condition. Any undefined condition. If for any undefined reason it is considered safer. Her healthy body may be a condition. Their lack of faith in her healthy body may be an indication.

It was there, between the lines, and she hadn't seen it.

Would anyone see it? Would Rick Jenkins, Roland's worst student, the one who was always asking questions and posing objections with an arrogance unsupported by his performance in exams, would he see it there between the lines if he opened the textbook? But now the textbook isn't even there in the library; if he goes to look for it, looking for an answer to the gap in his notes, there'll be a space on the shelf. He'll have to turn away, and go back down the steps, back towards the city and the streetlights scattered like greasy crumbs.

What of Arleen Manning, the best student ever, the apple of all the lecturers' eyes? What would she make of it? And in the light of that, what would she make of the other: *There are those who consider that induction of labour, with its risks to both the mother and the foetus of excessive stimulation to the uterus, may carry as high a risk as, for instance, postmaturity, so that, on balance, it is safer not to interfere . . .*

Incisive, alert, she'd be immediately suspicious. She'd flip to the frontispiece and confirm her conclusion that the book is out of date, failing to take account of the latest technology, superseded by the Professor's lectures.

It was her own fault, giving in to her insatiable hunger, distorting the chart. She'd done that, no one else. She had given them an excuse. She should have been on her guard.

But what if you don't know what it is you've got to be on guard against? The last thing she'd expected, running home for safety, was the bird, there before her. She put a foot forward. The bird dipped its head. She drew back. The bird shifted, settled its feet, settled in for a wait. It looked away, turned its beak towards the sky, turned its back to her. She started forward. The wings flapped open, a black umbrella. Just a trick. The bird regained its balance. It knew without looking when she tried to get past. Beyond the roof, clouds bubbled out and down in the sky. In front, cutting the sky off, one ragged black bird.

'Zelda, what are you doing there? Come inside, it's starting to rain!' One or two enormous drops fell like bluebottles and made black spots on the path. Past the corner mother's blue apron lifted, a pale blue parachute. The bird flew off with a cackle. The corner of the house became a free passage.

But for how long? Red herrings, hidden meanings. You can't bury the bird, its soul flies up again; you can't bury all the spindles, there'll still be one hidden, closest to home, obsolete, forgotten, so strange it winks like a new invention, all that will be needed is one little prick . . .

The machine is bleeping. Someone's calling for help. It's late, it's evening, electric light is prising her eyes, it's late, it's time. The mass forces downwards, jammed between her bones, rupturing through the peeling tissues of her body. She must push.

'No, no, stop that!' Their voices are urgent: 'It's not time, control it!' They are shouting: 'For heaven's sake, girl, remember your breathing – quick breaths, quick breaths!'

She does it, she gets control – snip, cuts her head and shoulders away from the rest of her body, lifts them floating on shallow dog-pants. 'Good girl, well done.' She's their baby, their goody, their Frankenstein beauty. Oh, no, she's not, here's the urge: her body gels, gathers, and now she's her very own monster, wolf-mouth howling, frog-legs flexing: they flinch back. She can make them flinch back, hold them off from her own magic circle. She laughs, wild strangled laughter, coiling helter-skelter inside the huge knot of her, she sees them looking from one to the other. In spite of their magic, in spite of their enemas, she squirts shit in their faces.

The head smashes down through the bag of her

abdomen. It won't come. It won't come out. Skull like a turnip, the enormous great big turnip that the farmer couldn't pull from the cold black earth. He pulled and pulled, but it wouldn't come up. The farmer called his wife. Sister calls Doctor. Doctor hears, Doctor sees. 'Foetal distress,' says Doctor; Foetal distress, said the textbook in its outdated type on good old-fashioned paper; 'Foetal distress,' calls the nurse. Sister calls the hospital porter. The farmer's wife called the boy. The doctor raises a syringe and plunges the needle into Zelda's arm.

They lift her over. The ceiling slips, she's slipping, losing her grip, losing substance, a soul that doesn't need feeding, falling, parachuting over the skull and round it and away, and for a moment she thinks she's free, that she's left it behind, bloody skull floating away above her. But then she sees the wild roses, coming towards her, a bank of pink roses, she's falling towards it, nearer and nearer, so close she can see the individual blossoms, five petals each, each petal shaped like a heart, pink at the outer edge, icy-white in the centre, the stamens bristling like unknown insects, and then she knows the time has come, to take Hilary's hand and scrabble in through the entrance, and the skull will be there, smashed up, bloody, not the doll's skull, but a real one.

Thirteen

SHE SITS UP. Unhinges her head and shoulders from the rest of her body, unclips them easily. Green underwater light fills the room. As she floats, swims up, she sees that the light is coming off the gowns, and from the sheet that covers this side of the belly she's left behind on the table. In the air is a low fallen watery sun. The gowned figures bend, engrossed. Are they speaking? She can't hear anything. The green light floats into her ears, blotting up the sound, and the white masks they are wearing hide any movement their lips might be making. To the left, one of them, guarding tall cylinders, touches her wrist. Her arm lies, white as a bone, by the side of the mound. He looks up towards the group at the foot of the table. One of them nods. Did they speak? She heard nothing. And then they all raise their heads and look in her direction. They have seen her, they have guessed. They have noticed what she's done. The tall one, the chief one, is making an amoeboid movement of his mask. He is speaking. What is he saying? And then she knows it's not her, it's someone else he's speaking to. She looks down, over her right shoulder, and sees that someone is sitting on the right at the head of the table, next to where her head and shoulders would be if they had not floated up. The head is capped with puffy linen like a Christmas pudding. A flash of glasses. Roland.

'Roland!' she calls down. 'Roland, you got here!'

He doesn't answer. Why not?

'Roland!' Her voice is loud and clear, making her jump, enough to make everyone else's head and shoulders jump from their bodies.

He hasn't even looked up. He stays fixed, his eyes directed towards the bottom of the table. What can he see? He must see nothing, everything is hidden, simply this side of the mound, green-sheeted and blank, and their hands and forearms dipping behind it, two doctors, one each side.

'Roland!' she calls.

No reply.

She floats out, changing her position to attract his attention, moves over his head, puffed linen collapsed where he's just reached up and scratched – a habit he has when he's nervous or awkward – a steamed pudding off the boil.

Out here, in the dimness, beyond the arc of the light, the sun can be seen to be drooping on a stalk. She can see Roland's face, but still he doesn't notice her. And now she sees there's someone else, standing back in the shadow, someone not wearing a surgical gown. Hilary. She moves from foot to foot. Her fuzzy hair shifts in the dimness. From where she is, she must have a very good view of what's going on. She steps forward, craning, her cardigan hanging, her knee-socks wrinkled, unscrubbed, gownless. It's this which rouses Roland. He starts in outrage, turns to complain, and catches sight of Zelda.

'Oh, Roland, what took you so long?'

His eyes are full, shiny humbugs. Poor Roland, it's hard to take, it must be an ordeal for him sitting in on this. He'll be expected to be brave. He'll be expected to want to. He is specially privileged. And yet he'll be expected to be especially grateful: think of what's at stake for this surgeon, in performing an operation in front of a colleague, on the colleague's own wife! The threat of critical observation overlaid with emotional involvement. He's a brave man, this surgeon. Zelda floats up to take a closer look at him. He's young, most likely Roland's age, an equal rival. His maskelastic is hooked around very large ears, and the white gauze flutters as he breathes intently. Brave, and generous, laying himself so open so that Roland can have his emotional fulfilment on this intimate occasion: under threat in such a way himself, he'll take it for granted that Roland will be brave, which gives Roland not the slightest leeway for the faintest flicker. Another pressure on Roland. Poor Roland. He must feel sick. Snip, snip.

The sound has come on. Snip, snip. A faint hum, like a generator. The surgeon murmurs to the attendant: 'Hold it there.' The attendant reaches, gown and plastic rustle. A nurse knocks a tray, and metal tinkles. Roland jumps. He's on edge.

What took him so long?

'It's the traffic, Zelda. You know very well it's now impossible to cross the city without coming to a sewer.'

'But, Roland, twelve hours! What happened, did you fall in?'

'What do you mean, twelve hours? I came twice, but both times you were asleep.'

'Well, couldn't you wake me?'

'Zelda, are you attacking me?'

'No. But why couldn't you wake me?'

'You *are* attacking me.'

'Well, why didn't you?'

'Because they advised me not to.'

'Oh.'

'Are you trying to row, at this moment, of all times?'

'No.'

He turns away and concentrates on the surgeon.

'But Roland, you should have, there were things I had to ask you, there were things I had to tell you.' How could he have cheated her of the knowledge he was there? She wants to prod him, he can't seem to hear her again, she wants to shake him, make him turn and confront her. But of course, she's got no arms.

The surgeon murmurs, 'More swabs,' and the nurse dabs. There must be blood, but she and Roland can't see over the mound.

They are present, they are here, but they are watching from a distance.

Of the three of them not involved, Hilary must have by far the best view.

'What's she doing here?' says Roland irritably. 'Look, she isn't scrubbed up, she isn't aseptic, she's a hazard, send her home.'

Hilary cranes, and ignores him. Her neck is ringed with grey, perfect joins between her head and her body. She's not afraid to peer, she's not afraid of blood.

Even the bird didn't frighten Hilary.

'Run!' she said. 'Now!'

Zelda willed the springs in her knees, but her feet remained planted. The bird turned on its feet, spun full circle, music-box bird, let it wind right down and the house roof would spring open.

'Now!'

She tore her feet off the ground, flung her body past the wall, she got round, with the bird looking down at her, driving down with its nail-head stare. She shut the door. She was in.

But the bird was on the roof. She was trapped inside now.

'Where have you been?' Mother was savage. 'Your father's out looking. Everyone's looking.' She knelt, seized Zelda's shoulders, pinned her with her eyes. She knew. 'Tell the truth. Where have you been?'

'In the woods.'

'Who've you been with?'

'Hilary.'

'Who else?' Mother's fingers dug.

'No one. Just Hilary.'

Mother's gaze faltered, swam, dropped, rose again to be sure. Then she stood and said curtly: 'Go upstairs and wash your hands.'

Did she know?

Zelda ran the water, sank her hands into the bowl. Her hands turned blue. Her forearms bent at the point where they went beneath the water. The bird scratched on the roof, turning once, threatening, a screw that could loosen and let the lid off.

The surgeon pauses; looks up at Roland, his surgical scissors poised. 'We're doing a transverse incision.'

'Oh,' says Roland, 'Good.'

Oh, good. A transverse incision. More commonly known as a bikini-line incision. Performed on those patients the obstetrician considers would otherwise suffer a reduction in their sexual viability. Oh, good. Now Zelda will be able to wander half-clad on beaches, her sexual viability intact. No one need know. No one will guess she's been through all this.

The surgeon goes on: 'We often don't bother in such cases, when it's a question of urgency, but we've managed this time.'

'Oh,' says Roland. 'Marvellous.' Marvellous. Specially for Roland.

'We're getting it nice and low, below the pubic hairline.' Oh, good. This surgeon must consider she wears very brief bikinis. This patient is a very sexy patient. Or so he flatters Roland.

He busies himself cutting.

Hilary moves in and looks over his shoulder.

Zelda says to Hilary: 'Did you ever tell them?'

Hilary looks up, and asks, 'Did you?'

Never. The bird stopped her, a morse-code warning over

the ceiling. She hung back on the landing. 'Zelda!' Mother knew she was there.

'Are your hands clean?'

'Yes.'

'Then come on down, we want to talk to you.'

She knew that. From an upstairs window she had seen the car skimming up the lane, electric-blue flashing.

The drivers were waiting in the living room, dark stiff crocodiles, all down their bodies hard knuckles of silver.

She flinched in the doorway, all her soft flesh cringing.

'Don't be frightened, little girl. Come on in.'

Mother nodded. Zelda must obey. She came in, wincing through the invisible trip wire.

'Who do you play with, Zelda?'

'Hilary.'

'With anyone else?'

No. No one else. She looked from one to the other. The policeman looked at mother. Did mother give a signal? The policeman turned his hat in his hands, a black disc, round and round, full circle and back again. Measuring something.

'Don't you have any other friends?'

No. Only Hilary.

Mother said, 'What about the other girl, and the little boy?'

'Oh, no. Not for a long time. No, not for ages.'

They paused, exchanging glances, stringing them across, over her head, weaving a net.

'Where were you this afternoon?'

'In the woods.'

'Who with?'

'Hilary.'

'No one else?'

'No.'

'Did you see anyone?'

The bird tapped: Don't you dare. The witch's bird flew down, flicked across the window.

'No, no one,' said Zelda. 'I didn't see anyone.'

'OK.' They stood. Their metal bodies untelescoped, loomed, pushed out the spaces of the room. Zelda drew back, put her arms behind her, shielded their flesh, the pink-and-white skin, a thin skin that could be broken to let out red blood.

The attendant clips the blood off, clamps the vessels. They've worked right across; now the surgeon must lean a little, and the attendant no longer has to. Someone's stomach rumbles. It's getting late. Someone needs their supper.

'Nearly there,' says the surgeon.

The attendant stands back. Now it's up to the chief, to put his hand in and deliver. 'Oh!' he says, conversationally, just before he pulls, 'I can see it's a boy!'

A boy. Good Lord, a boy. She hadn't imagined the possibility of a boy.

The boy. Who would have guessed it would be the boy, under the pink-and-white skin of roses?

A sluther. Pop. He pulls it out, like a rabbit from a hat.

A purple corkscrew baby.

'There we are, it's a boy!' He holds it up for all to see, in his two plastic hands: bent and raw, the prune scrotum hanging. It blinks and stares, black currants of surprise.

'Here, Dad!' says the surgeon, and hands the baby to Roland.

Roland holds out his arms, stiff, bent in the middle – Meccano arms. Be careful, Roland, the baby will drop out of them. 'Hello,' says Roland. To the baby, experimentally. 'Hello,' in a strange, thin, puppet-on-a-string voice, looking up briefly, aware of people watching him. 'Hello.'

The baby stares, shocked.

'All right, Dad,' says a nurse, coming up behind Roland,

'we mustn't let him get cold.' Dad must be quickly relieved of the baby; Dad is overwhelmed, as Dads can be expected to be on such occasions. Roland tries to hand the baby over. There's a struggle, arms tangled – should he straighten or bend them? Then the nurse gets the baby and bears it away.

'Right!' says the surgeon, and begins quickly sewing up the incision. Zelda looks down. Her stomach has gone flat. Back to normal. Transformed. Abracadabra. Good as new. He sews quickly, magic stitches that disappear all by themselves in a week. Invisible mending. No one will know.

Zelda stood by the garden wall. The marjoram bristled with flower buds. Marjoram, meant for the easing of the spirits. Zelda kept looking up. Over the wall, the other side of the lane. Beyond that, the hill, and at the top the crust of trees. She waited for the figures to appear at the top, distant, cutout. The men had found the place. The police had gone in a party. Close to, maroon buds like blood clots. She watched for the men to bring down the cold body.

The baby has gone. They have taken it away. And she hasn't even touched it. They handed it to Roland. Not to her.

Of course. She should never have detached her head and shoulders from her body.

Fourteen

Roland relaxes. That's that. All sewn up. A sense of fulfilment, patterns completed. The surgeon makes neat stitches.

Then Roland groans. He's suddenly remembered. 'What's she doing here, at a time like this?'

He folds his arms, perking up, and turns intently to Zelda. 'You know one of your main problems, Zelda? You just can't keep your mind on a thing. I mean, you have to confess it illustrates a certain lack of concentration on the matter in hand!' He flings a hand in Hilary's direction.

Hilary is now right up against the surgeon, almost getting in his way, in fact. Her eyes make circular motions, following the path of the needle as it swoops. As Roland finishes speaking, she looks blandly at him and blinks.

He lets out a spout of exasperation, and shoots his arms together again, dives them into each other. One comes out again immediately, the hand begins to jab the air with little bird-like swoops to illustrate his argument.

'I mean, I forgive you your untidy mind, your spurious connections – I've learnt to live with them a long time ago, but for heaven's sake, Zelda, this makes me start to wonder about your basic *humanity!* I mean, for heaven's sake, one would have expected you, at a time like this, to have found it hard to think about much else beside the *baby!*' (Oh, yes, the baby, what did it look like? It's gone, she's forgotten.) 'Zelda, are you listening?'

'Yes, Roland.'

'Well, then.' Roland rests his case. He folds his arms.

'Roland?'

'Yes, Zelda?' He's calmer now, kinder, he can afford to understand her. Hilary's looking curiously from one to the other.

'Are you saying she's a figment of my imagination?'

'Well, of course!' He looks at Hilary contemptuously. 'Well, yes!'

Hilary grins back.

Roland falters.

Who's imagining what? Did she really see the baby? It came and went so quickly . . .

The nurse scoops the swabs into the bin, red-and-pink petals. Look once, blink your eyes; they were there, they have gone. Look inside, blink your eyes: was it true, what she saw in the wood?

They held hands. Sun came down in warm drops. The shadows were black splashes. Insects droned. Something flying made wires of light in the shade and then landed on the roses. A black beetle crawled out of the petals, shook its legs from the tangle of stamens, stood shining and poised, felt the air with its quivering whiskers, and then took off. Winking life taking off, bristling life going on.

Yards away, something shifted. They hid themselves and watched as it separated out from the tree trunks, assembled itself into a bright patch of colour. Purple and yellow: a shape that was human. Legs, flapping clothes. A bright knitted helmet. A face that assumed the features of a troll. The witch. So that was it. She must have been there all the time, life behind the trees, watching and waiting. She turned now, walked off and away, out of the wood and down the hill.

All the time the evil promise had been working to its conclusion. But who'd have guessed the trick, who'd have guessed the inversion? Who'd have guessed it would be the boy who died?

Fifteen

Hilary has gone. Roland has gone. It is not the same room. She has been somewhere – swimming – she's come up out of the greenness, the darkness, and is in a grey room.

She is pinned again, trapped. A drip is in her left arm. What time of day? Grey light across the ceiling. A room, a bed, a dull plastic tube. Are those bubbles in the tube? Bubbles in the lifeline, bubbles of death?

She closes her eyes, sinks down through black water, groping, reaching for something, and hits the bottom, and then she grasps it: the memory, the picture, of the head of the baby. That was it. It had only one eye. No nose. Its eye folded inwards to the centre, and the single eye looking out, like the eye of a bean.

She struggles up, out. The surface splits, grey light flaps down. A nurse is leaning above. No. She was wrong. There were two eyes. She remembers. The image bobs on the surface of consciousness. Real life. A real room. A real nurse: her hand is warm.

'Would you like to sit up?' She plumps the pillows: warm breath on Zelda's neck. But the face, the head and shoulders of the nurse, they float, cardboard cutout, difficult to register.

The baby's face bobs under. She pulls it back. Yes, there: two currants of surprise, two dots of disbelief. Disbelief. The image sinks. There's the other, bean-shape, white-eye, floating under the surface. Somewhere, in the distance, there are birds calling.

When the lorries started up, the birds rose, rain reversed, shooting back into the sky. Then, over the churning mud, white birds assembled from out of the air, a suspended snow cloud, undulating, screaming, dissolving back once the engines were silent for the night, and the mud had gone cold.

After the body of the boy had been found, they kept the children indoors. It wasn't safe. She had to stay inside and find indoor things to do. Father brought a sheet of paper, one of his old ones: she could draw on the back. She sat at his desk by the window, her coloured crayons laid out before her.

She would draw a row of shops. She made two lines, straight across: the roof, enclosed and compact. Then the shop front and the pavement: more lines, the whole strung, anchored on the edges of the sheet. Then the wares. Flowers in the florist's: daisies, neat halos in buckets, pink, blue and yellow; meat in the butcher's, firm marks of punctuation, large red commas on small question-mark hooks, each coiled round a central knucklebone. What colour was the bone? White? No, it had a sheen, and shifting pearly colours, pink and blue. How could she do that with crayons? The crayon colours were solid, obvious, unmagic. There wasn't even a white. With a sense of disappointment, she left a hole for the bone, a hole of naked paper in a red surround of crayon.

The fish in the fishmonger's. Green and blue, as she'd always imagined. It didn't work. They looked flat, like cutout fishes, it looked as though her fishmonger sold bits of felt for fishes. And each fish too must have a hole to represent the gleam of its eye. A staring hole. Blank. Like an error. Like a piece forgotten.

She turned the sheet over, and Father's spidery drawings

were there like quiet ghosts. Outside the window, birds, real birds, dropped across the sky. They called, throwing lines of sound across the blue, secret messages, or warnings. It wasn't safe out of doors. Only with mother, along permissible ways, straight tarmac roads, to the village for shopping.

Until one morning, when Mother and Zelda, keeping close together, came towards the village square. A group of women huddled on one corner, gesturing and nudging, looking over their shoulders towards the Police House, where three bluebottle cars basked in the heat. The Police House baked, its bricks biscuit-brown. The air was silent. No bird-scream. The women were talking, you could see their mouths moving, but no sound carried. They turned and saw Mother and Zelda, all their faces blank sheets of paper, ready to be drawn on. Mother and Zelda crossed the tarmac towards them, a grey pool that seemed to spread as they walked. They kept going. The women waited. Someone spoke.

The voice rang. 'They've found the one.' One-one, the voice echoed, the air was hollow, the day was emptied, its contents tipped away. No birds calling.

But the biscuit-house was throbbing. The woman jerked her head. In there was the one. Handcuffed, arrested. Zelda imagined: rings of metal round those wrists, black-pudding fingers dangling, powerless. Could the enchantment be broken with two metal rings? The voices rattled. There'd been a house-to-house search. Policemen coming up the path, black feet on white stone, shoe-stud sounding on rock, striding into a circle of air warm with the smell of baking. And banging on the door, wooden slats like strips of angelica, peering through the icing lace curtains, standing back, looking round at the rock-bun stones. Come out, old witch, we know you are there, we can smell your baking. Birds on the roof looking down, silent as the stones, waiting for the men to cut into the house like a crumbly cake.

Up on the bank, the door opened in the Police House. The women started, stood back, got ready to ogle. The door swung, winked in the sun, and then was pushed to again from behind. A pause. A hitch. They weren't coming out yet. Of course: old ladies can stumble. Witches can trick, can trip people up. How much power is left when the hands are encircled?

Then the door winked again, pulled inwards to let people out. Another pause. A gaping hole. Someone emerged. A policeman, silver buttons. He stepped out, down, separated out from the blackness, became a dark figure against the bright day. He stood aside to let the rest out; two figures together, one dark, one coloured. Handcuffed together. Zelda stared. The coloured figure was tall, as tall as the policeman. The coloured figure was a man.

They came out into the sunshine, and brightness leapt from the prisoner: red from the shirt, orangey-tan from the skin, and tawny yellow out of the hair. He screwed his face, dazzled, and showed a line of blue-white teeth.

A man. A man she had seen before. Had he seen her, that other time, the time she wore a front of red mud? Could he see her now? She stood behind the women. The women stirred, quietly, excited, frightened, whispering: There he is, there's the one, they interviewed all the men, all the workers on the site, and there's the one they found: not a monster, not a troll, but a handsome young man.

They led him down the path. More policemen followed. They pushed a little, jerked, he stumbled, they righted him quickly. They opened the car doors, black doors, swinging, banging – birds flying up now with all the commotion, wheeling in confusion, falling like oil drops, rising up again as engines started, the sky teetering with flight, rooftops skewed, tipping into the distance, not balanced after all, as you'd always imagined.

A trick within the prophecy.

A boy, not a girl. A man, not a witch.

The birds screamed with derision.

She opens her eyes. The birds are still calling. One, then another, an elongated thread of sound that picks up another and draws it behind it; more threads spinning under them, then the whole together, a tangle of sound. Where are they, the birds? Above is a ceiling; where are they, on the roof? To the right, a patch of sky beyond glass, but nothing moves, there are no birds circling.

They are inside. She knows it suddenly. The birds have come in. They are in the building. Trapped souls, lost souls, floating in the corridors.

The nurse comes. 'Let the birds out,' says Zelda, 'let them out, they are trapped, they are frightened, they'll rip us alive.'

'What, dear?' The nurse touches Zelda. Warm hands.

'What's that noise?'

'What noise?'

Can't she hear it? There it is: scratching, up and down, loops of sound shuttling.

'That! That sound like birds calling!' She grabs the nurse's arm.

The nurse listens, puzzled. Then she knows, she adjusts. 'Oh, *that!* That's the babies, in the nursery. That's the babies crying.'

Babies crying. 'Oh,' says Zelda.

Someone's drawing up a syringe. Someone's taking her arm. Someone's pressing a needle into the crook of her arm.

Babies. The greenness swims over. Babies crying. She calls up through the water: 'Is one of them mine?'

But no, a monster wouldn't cry. The deep blackness comes up. The monster couldn't, wouldn't be able to. That face was all eye, blank whiteness, and the fold below it just a fold, no mouth that could open to let out a cry. Dumb.

Sleeping and staring. Almost dead. Lost, irreparably damaged. Locked in an irreversible spell.

And she has done it.

Sixteen

YES, SHE HAS done it. Because of her sins, her child is damaged. Right at the beginning, she sowed the seeds of death. Her mistake, her arrogance, was to assume she couldn't hurt, to assume she had the power to protect. She made that same mistake twice.

The first time she thought: He won't know. I can protect him from knowledge that would hurt him. But of course Roland knew, he knew enough to be uneasy. He noticed her body. He looked at her naked, he noticed her clothed. He said, 'You're looking good.' He said, 'You've lost weight.'

Well, of course she'd lost weight. She had almost stopped eating. She'd lost interest in food. She couldn't cook, she couldn't concentrate, she forgot the salt, she failed to turn on the heat. She was full of her secret; she had no appetite left for cooking or for eating. Did she ever consider where it would end? No, she drew a veil over Roland, she saw him through gauze. And that, of course, was another way he knew: her heightened behaviour, her unreal daydream manner.

In the end he asked her point-blank.

His brown eyes trembled. He couldn't face the truth he had guessed. He blinked. He gasped, drowning in air, in the cold air of truth.

'Don't leave me, Zelda.' He reached out, he grasped her arms, his eyes two brown circles of pleading, two brown circles of disbelief.

She went cold. She couldn't cope. She stood still, unresponding. She had nothing to give him. In dismay she watched him flounder, watched him register her coldness, drop his arms, lift them briefly again, and finally collapse, double up, sobbing.

He came to her later, his eyes red with weeping.

'Zelda.' His voice cracked on her name. He stood at a distance. He wouldn't touch her. He dared not. He stood, lost, knowing his place outside her enchanted circle. His hands hung, helpless.

'Zelda, say it doesn't matter, say it doesn't mean anything. Tell me it's just a passing affair.' His voice had no power, a mere whisper. All the power was hers, to dispel, or not, as she chose, the magic ring. She heard the childlike croak of his voice; she thought of him earlier, doubled up, foetal, over his grief; she couldn't bear it. Out of grief that things were as they were, out of longing that they should not be, she said: 'Oh, Roland, yes!' And she held out her hands, and the circle broke down, and Roland came in, and she hugged him to her. And his body was stiff in her arms, and the wool of his jumper coarse, like wire.

Roland said: 'I can love you like that. I can love you like he can.' His eyes swerved, desperate, grasping for the secret. What was it she had wanted? What was it she had got that he must learn to give her?

'There was no need,' he said, repeating it, over and over, stroking her arm up and down, up and down: 'I can love you like that.'

She let her hand trace his troubled, dark-skinned face. She felt: perhaps for his wanting to, she could really love him, as she'd loved the other. If for nothing else, for his so desperately wanting to, she ought to love him. His hand, moving up and down, made the hairs on her arm stand on end.

He would try the same formulae. He would try the

same forms. The perfect, time-honoured forms. Food, paid for highly, in a ritual setting. He took her out to dinner.

They had pheasant with cream. They ought to, said Roland, it was the end of the season, it would be the last chance. The dish gleamed with sauce, a smothered hump in the mud-coloured sauce, the surprise of the elbow poking up, a jagged reminder of the animal form. The last of the season, the last of a bone-hard, wind-swept winter, rotten and sweet with the taste of long hanging. The sauce parted in the crook of the elbow, the leg, and left a hole, a blank eye.

And compôte of root vegetable, the last and the biggest, sour and musty, the longest buried in the cold black earth. The wine, meant to be white, lapped green in the glass, gathering, when it was moved, small black shadows, like spores drawn in then dissolved. It stank faintly like mould.

'All right?' said Roland, 'Is everything all right?' He was anxious. He couldn't relish the food any more than she could, he must feel queasy as she did. 'All right?' He reached across the table.

He took her hand. The time-honoured gesture, the formulaic signal, hands-across-the-table, signature tune, tune-on-the-brain, recorded, round and round for ever, reproduced, dry icon, bone-fingers, dust hands on the table.

She must protect him. At once. From her disgust. From her weary disgust. At once. And forever. She moved her hand out from under his, and placed it back on top, stroking to and fro, soothing, there-there, it's all right, everything's going to be all right. She would love him, she could love him, enough, in her way, for the things he could be loved for, and everything was going to be all right. She stroked, to and fro, there-there, it's all right; he looked up, his eyes flickered with hope, he moved his thumb to and fro in response.

'It was a mistake,' said Roland. 'A misunderstanding. I

didn't know. I didn't know what you wanted. I can love you like he can.'

He would make love to her differently. Away from the marriage bed. He undressed her slowly. He took her scarf at one end. He pulled. The knot unravelled, the snake of it uncoiled and slipped to her feet. He kissed her neck. Slowly, deliberately, he undid the buttons of her blouse. As each fastening fell apart, he dropped his face and placed a kiss, marking the progression. Bit by bit, the clothes peeled off, and on each new space he imprinted a kiss. Cold kisses. His lips were cold. She shivered. Her body froze, her unpicked body, torso naked to the waist, cold female statue. She would not be ready for love. She would disappoint, dismay. Fail to protect him. She drew his head to her breasts and rocked him to and fro.

And then she realised he was weeping: her breasts were wet with his tears, warm fluid substance of his emotion. At that she was ready, she too became flesh that could weep. She could fall, sink back, take him in, the dark full root of him, enclose him round, love him. Her body unfolded in widening spaces, endless space he could enter and never once hurt her.

She closed her eyes. Now there was darkness. Now she was in the darkness with him. He moved, she moved to meet him, across the spaces she had made for him, to and fro, soothing, there-there, everything all right now. She clasped him round, rocked him.

Without warning, his movement changed. She was used to this; his final uncontrolled burst. She waited. It wasn't the same. No quickening rush towards the sudden end. Measured. Her eyes opened, the light clicked into her head. Outside was the room. Yellow light, and music still playing on the stereo. Round and round, music on a machine, signature music, everybody's music, anybody's music, familiar, patterned. Measured. He was moving in time to the music.

Inside her, up and down, repeating the pattern, everybody's pattern, beating a tattoo on the core of her body. Her body on the floor, half-clad like a body in a painting, anybody's painting. They were bodies merely, dead bodies, dust bodies, they touched each other and turned to dust.

No, no, that wasn't true, she couldn't bear it to be true. She had the power to heal it. He needn't know, she could protect him from the truth of it. She could understand his need, his weakness. She would nourish him out of it, and so cancel the truth of it.

She shut her eyes, shut out the light. She put her arms round him as he moved still, rhythmically, deliberately, she drew her hands across his cold faint greasiness. Something floated in the darkness: his waxy skin, his death-white body. She squeezed her eyes, wrung the image from the darkness.

The same mistake, a second time: to bury things, to dig the images over, sew them up. She had even forgotten. She thought she had forgotten.

They come back now. She remembers.

She remembers how, at the end, he stood, quickly, crossed the room, naked, turned the record over, and came back and said: 'The thing that would make me happiest of all, would be if you were pregnant now.'

And as it turned out, she was.

And the other: she pushed him under, down below the surface.

Something bobs. On the watery surface. A live thing going down and coming up again. Like a kidney. Something partial. Unformed. With an eye, a single eye. White, staring, unseeing. She struggles to escape. It bobs along on the current, moving towards her. She flails, choking, to get away. At last it recedes, disappearing, reappearing, tiny, alone. She could have saved it, and she's lost it, it's lost and alone, floating for ever. She is weeping, on dry land. There are flowers.

'Mrs Harris! Flowers!'

A hand above the bed holds out a glass vase. Flowers in the air, above her body. Flowers, arranged. She stares. Neat flowers, in a pattern. Each one a fluted tube. The shape repeated from one to the other. But different colours. Red, yellow and blue. What are they, these flowers? Does she know them, their name? Flowers without sepals, naked, waxy, like painted lilies. She knew their name once, she lost it, she has no name to redeem them; call them what you like, the real name is lost, no other name will redeem them. They float, alien, unreal, flowers without leaves, cut flowers, lopped, separated from the earth. They float, through the air, sideways, and settle on a table, precarious and sinister, divested of their name.

She has lost all the names, the names of the birds: they fly up without them, set loose, out of control, spinning off into frightening spaces, coming back with threatening secrets. There's one now, screaming into the corridor, coming back, coming in . . .

No. She remembers. It's the cry of a baby.

'Nurse!'

The nurse turns back. Yes, here she is. A nurse, warm and intact, coming back to answer, to cross the room. Yes, here's the room, and here's the bed, and there's the sound, coming in through the open door, a sobbing, squalling sound, human, the cry of a baby.

She was right. It was two eyes, not one. Pink features, proper features, anchored on two dark round stones.

'Nurse, is that my baby crying?'

'No. Oh, no, no.' The nurse scoops the blankets, tidies them under, brushes Zelda's hair from her forehead. 'No, no. Don't you worry. It's not yours, go to sleep now.'

How did she know? How could the nurse know

without looking? Of course. They all know. She knows, too, but she'd forgotten, got it wrong for a moment.

A mouthless face cannot cry.

Seventeen

Two dots, a dash, a half-circle like a moon. The face of the butcher. Mother hovered, pretending not to, clattering dishes, watching over her shoulder while she drew.

Rib-mouth butcher: Roll up, roll up, Ladies and Gentlemen, meat for your frying pan, joints for your stoves, come and buy, come and taste my wares. Stiff-mouth, he'd never taste them himself, all those bits of bodies hanging, pencil-mouth, he'd never really say it: 'Come and see, come and buy, live bodies rendered dead.'

She drew the fishmonger's features: upside-down moon. Melancholy fishmonger above his dead scraps of fish. The picture was growing, every day she added something, the page was packed tighter, getting stiffer with drawings.

Late at night she heard them talking about it.

'She just sits there,' said Mother, 'day after day, with the very same drawing. I don't know what's got into her.'

Mother paused. She'd be undoing the hooks at the back of her skirt. Father's braces clattered on the chair. They were going to bed. Still silence, while Mother concentrated. Zelda could picture her hands, curled backwards towards each other, fumbling from underneath, groping for the tight black bits of metal: insects, interlocked, that must be prised from each other.

Then she did it. She went on: 'She says nothing – you know: about all that business. I've tried once or twice to give her an opening. But no – not a word.'

Father grunted. There was a swish as he turned back the bedclothes. Two creaks, one prolonged, the second shorter and lighter, as first Father, then Mother got into bed and settled.

'You wouldn't even think,' said Mother, 'she'd ever known the boy, that she'd ever had anything to do with him at all.'

They didn't know. They'd no idea. That soon the picture would be finished, and she'd roll it up then, and put it away.

She heard their bodies writhing.

All around there's a rustling. She wakes up. They want her sitting, they are propping her up, hands under her legs, arms linked across her back. They lift; bend her body. Pain slices right across her. She gasps, to cry out, but the pain grabs, pulls the breath back down again. They heave, slide her further up the bed. The knife bites. The cry escapes. They stand back. They are disapproving. She shouldn't cry. She must be brave. She's had plenty of painkillers, she can't have any more; she's had the full dosage, the magic formula, the pain can't be that bad. There-there, it's all right, it's not as bad as she thinks. They push wadding at her back.

They stroke her hair, they lift it up from her forehead, lift it off, prop it back.

'That's a good girl; will you do a wee for us now?'

They must lift her again, to get her on the bedpan. One must take the weight while the other slips the bedpan under. They lift, she's leaned sideways; the pain catches and freezes. If she moves to straighten it will overwhelm her. She's stuck, knocked sideways.

'There we are. Have a try. Come on, can you wee?'

No, nothing. No sensation below the waist but the sharp, suspended pain.

'Come on, sit straighter.' They push her up, prise her. The pain tears through her. Nothing. No water. This is not a body that will pass out water. Bad veins, bad placenta, inadequate bladder. No blood. No water.

They take her off, let her down, tight-lipped, they take the pan away empty.

On the table there are flowers. More than before. The same kind: coloured trumpets. Who sent them? Did they say? Did they tell her the name of the sender? Who sent a message for flowers over the telephone? Who spoke, who said the word, the name of these flowers, and the word became signals in a wire spun across the sky where the birds fly circling?

A nurse enters, talking over her shoulder. A doctor replies: 'No, it's OK, no problem, we'll give her something stronger. We'll get her through today, it doesn't matter if she's out, she's not feeding, is she?'

A needle sinks into her arm.

Who said that? Who said 'No'? 'No, she's not feeding'? What do they mean? Do they mean not eating? Not feeding. Feeding what? The baby. They mean the baby.

The birds fly up off the wires, screaming with hilarity; 'Baby,' they are calling, 'baby-aby,' distorting the sound of it, of course she's not feeding, how can you feed a thing without a mouth? With a slit that goes nowhere? The milk would just dribble off the chinless face, over the strange curled lizardy body. The birds scream with laughter, stretching reptile mouths, beating the air with pterodactyl wings, zooming in with lizardy grins. Not that. She blots it out. Struggles back:

'Nurse, Nurse, that's not right, I want to feed my baby.'

The water surges. She falls back. How could she, how silly, how could she ever get the nipple in?

Fill the blanks. Cover the empty spaces. More flowers in the flower shop. Cram the window: more daisies; and roses, each with five neat queen-of-heart petals. Fill the fish shop with people, square heads, straight noses, one eye staring from sideways. Crowd them in, pack them tight, push the spaces under. Soon the paper would be covered, like wrapping paper, not a picture after all, but a stiff solid pattern, that was better than the throbbing empty spaces. Then she'd put it away. She'd put it under the stairs.

But in the end, when she'd finished and she pushed it under, as she shut the cupboard door, she knew that wasn't the answer.

She pushes, thrusts at the blackness. She comes up. The room opens out, curtain up, lights up, everything bright and sharp as a pantomime. She turns her head. Something round on the wall at her side: a black dome with a central white nipple. A bell. A bell she can ring if she stretches, if she brings her free arm over her body, leans sideways and presses. She hasn't seen it before. Was it there before? The magic button. Open Sesame.

She stretches. No pain. The pain's gone. She presses the bell. She takes her finger away. The white nipple jumps back, shining, polished. An enormous figure towers by her bed.

'Yes?' It's a girl. A young nurse. Dun-coloured overall. 'Yes?' she says, sullen as a waitress in a short-order café.

'I want my baby. I want to feed him. I must feed him. Now.'

The girl has gone. Did she hear? Has she gone to get him? Is it a trick? Will she return?

Zelda struggles, half-sits. No pain.

The girl appears in the doorway. Yes, she's come back. And in her arms there's a bundle, stiff and swathed, a small mummy. Is the baby inside it? Zelda puts her hands out and leans forward. The pain jumps up, an iron bar forcing her backwards. The girl advances, and dumps the bundle. It rolls on Zelda's stomach. The face is turned away, the ear and chin are hidden by the cloth, all that's visible is one closed eye in profile. She strains to pull herself up and draw the baby to her. Her hands crumple on thick arms. The girl has hold of the baby.

'Let go,' she says. 'Let go, let me have him.'

'No,' says the girl. 'No.' Her brown eyes are dark and stubborn.

'I'll hold him. You undo your buttons.'

Zelda fumbles with the fastenings. White lips of cloth seem to yield, then fold again over the openings. The cold drip-tube catches in the crook of her arm.

'Come on,' says the girl. She looks over her shoulder. There's a squeak, a snuffle, inside the swaddling.

'There,' says Zelda. Her breast is exposed, beginning to tingle for the baby to be brought across the space between them. Turn him round, turn his face, two eyes and a mouth that will soothe the tingling. 'Let me hold him.'

'No. I must help you.'

The girl keeps hold, and turns the baby, tips him over, and the face turns to Zelda. Two eyes. Two dark eyes. It's all right. There, there. The girl pushes, the mouth grazes. It misses the nipple. The face slips, down and sideways, one-eye profile. Zelda braces to lift it back. But the girl is pushing sternly, and the drip-tube tangles and knocks the skewed baby's head, and through the numbness of her hand Zelda can feel the catheter dragging.

The girl looks quickly behind her. She's going red, she's hot and bothered, her voice is gruff with irritation: 'Come on!'

Zelda must move, adjust her body to fit the baby. She strains. She can't. She's trapped by the tube, the numbness and the pain. Again the girl glances back, why does she keep doing that? What is wrong? What's going on?

The girl snaps the baby back. 'It's no good.' She stands up. She's got the baby, she holds him to her, tucks the bundle under her large waxed bosom, with two red arms cradles it to her. She turns quickly, strides off, dumpy, her overall rustling.

But the baby was all right. She saw it, she won't forget it: two eyes.

The water sweeps, meets above her. She pulls the image, takes it down with her. Two eyes. She tucks it under her arm, warm sphere, two eyes, nestled to her rib cage. The water laps. Something knocks them in the darkness. What else is floating beside them? What is that nudging? She turns, treads water, faces about. Something bird-like, a reptile. An underwater lizard. The face opens and grins. Not that. She thrashes up, up and out.

The stage is lit. A voice is calling, off. 'Nurse! Auxiliary Nurse! What are you doing with that baby?'

A mumbled answer, the words indistinct.

'Come here, please!'

The girl appears in the doorway, fat girl, girl peasant, clutching her bundle like kindling, facing the accuser beyond the doorway.

The imperious voice: 'Nurse, are you aware that this patient is under sedation?'

Another mumble. The peasant girl hangs her head.

The queen-voice rings: 'In future, obey the instructions. That was not the right time. You must be more careful.'

That's it. It isn't hers. That's why the two-eyed baby didn't fit her body. They have swopped it, changed it over. Somewhere, still bobbing, is the face of the other.

Eighteen

Things gone wrong. Patterns inverted.

A simple start, a simple wish. A fish jumps, sperm-shape, comma in the flow of things, a simple movement, automatic, primordial. The fish blows a clean bubble. 'Oh, Lord and Lady, thy wish shall be granted.' The pastel lady starts. Her husband in the distance is gathering blue nettles. The bubble bursts. The prophecy scatters, to reassemble in a different pattern.

It was the trick of the prophecy, to disappear and reappear with a different meaning: that the child, being born, would be born to danger.

This, too, was a catch: that the evil lay in wait, not for a girl, but for a boy. According to expectation, it should not have been a boy. Two girls, they were prepared, they'd been brought up to know about danger, and so to expect it. To know themselves as vulnerable, to listen out, every so often to look over their shoulders.

On that day, that fatal day, Zelda and Hilary knew straightaway what it was when they heard the rustling in the bushes out beyond the roses: monstrosity, death, moving towards them, out to get them, to snuff out their lives, obliterate their bodies. They jumped up, they dashed out, they were ready to run.

'Hey!'

The voice was the boy's. Human, thin, mundane. That was all, just the boy, wanting to play. Fear dropped from their bodies and left them trembling. He'd moved away behind the trees, he didn't want them to know he'd been spying; there he was, just visible: brown clothes, mottled skin. Chameleon. Now he scrabbled back towards them. 'Hey! I saw Annie before, she said you didn't come here any more!' He was accusing, he obviously felt they were plotting against him. He looked around, expecting Annie to be somewhere nearby. Then, realising she wasn't, he kicked his heels, wondering.

He would tell.

'What're you doing in there?' His face split open, a straight gap between the freckles.

Had he seen?

He kicked the roots with his hobnail lace-ups, his crusted head turning and seeking to know what they'd been doing. Leather-skin. Lizard-boy. Go away. Stamp him out.

Instead, they walked off, took hands and left him all alone. Alone with the evil, which, after all, was still lurking in the wood. Removed themselves for one fatal half-hour. Left him there instead. Changed over.

They escaped. Because of that, he died.

A dimmed spotlight falls on a gleaming oblong. White cloth. A human shape embossed. A torso and legs. All around there are flowers, dark, waxed, nameless lilies, impotent symbols of a message on the sky. Zelda's arm is stretched, her hand still pinned. There's something else now: another stand at the foot of the bed, another plastic container. Another tube. This one snakes beneath the bedclothes. A urinary catheter. Along its length there are black-edged bubbles, air transformed into gleaming pebbles. She moves her leg; the tube swings, the bubbles rock, drop back towards the bed, float towards the spaces of her body. They stop, suspended. Death suspended.

She lies back. She can suffer. Without feelings, without needs, it is easier to suffer. No hunger. No urge in the bladder. The drip feeds, the catheter drains. She's a soul that can rise above her physical body. She has learnt to atone.

Nineteen

The need to atone. No washing of hands.

You couldn't dip them in the water, see them bend, turn blue, and wash away the secret. The bird was laughing on the roof. Father heard it, Father guessed. Let me see them, hold them up. She lifted pink-and-white palms, naked flesh that could be battered. He wasn't tricked. Turn them over. There it was beneath the nails, something dark and congealed.

He knew. He knew what she'd done. He knew she was guilty. He sent her back to scrub with a nailbrush. To cover up. But he knew. And the birds knew, too, souls flying up from iridescent puddles to circles and see, seizing the secret, flying back, taking it with them, diving back to the water, white-finned reptiles.

Silver fish flicker. One silver fish flicks its tail in the darkness. No. That's wrong. It's a baby's voice, crying. Is it hers, her baby? The one they brought her? Or is it another? The cry stops; she'll never know, the fish swims away, fluorescent dot going back into sea-bed blackness. It's gone, she's lost it forever.

Things lost forever. No redemption. The drawing: it had gone. When she next opened the cupboard, someone had removed it. Her symbols were vulnerable, impotent, easily dispelled by a careless hand.

What else is gone? Someone whispers, far away: 'You

remember.' No, no, it's gone, gone forever. A fish nibbles at her ear, the fish blows a bubble like a kiss: Here it is.

Here it is, the other memory. Rain-washed. Every leaf distinct. Cold fingers of grass touching their legs. The bushes swung vibrating arms and flicked their backs with tongues of water.

The wild roses had opened. As the sun warmed, insects buzzed and fluttered on their blinking stamens. Hilary and Zelda pulled at the entrance.

It was wrong. They did wrong. Where've you been, what's got into you, what have you been up to? Nothing. It never happened. Crush the memory.

The fish blows a bubble; the bubble floats into her ear, passes through the orifice and knocks inside her skull. The memory of a skull, someone else's battered skull. That memory isn't gone, it's always there, knocking, someone else's round skull knocking for ever and ever inside her own.

No, not that, the fish nibbles: another, different memory. The fish whispers. Here it is.

The roses winking. Surprises of cold as the branches swung back. Inside it was dim, and the ground had stayed dry. In the corner lay the doll, left to rot: just a doll, with a wormholed head they had filled with bubbles of decay.

They could bring her to life if they chose. Resurrect the cold plastic. Warm flesh at a touch.

Hilary's fingers fluttered like insects. Zelda's flesh tingled. The insects nuzzled, antennae tickling, wings brushing away her clothes. They wriggled down in the crevice. They fixed themselves, snuggled. They nudged together. They rocked. Her flesh swam, across her stomach, down her legs, in circular ripples. Then inside her, something jumped. Jumped again, over and over. The shudders faded and slipped away. She lay still. At last she moved, curled her liquid legs.

There was live hair on Hilary's body. It coiled, clasped,

finally parted. Hilary moaned. Her soft flesh throbbed. When Zelda lifted her hand, there was blood, petals.

Blood on her hands. Someone died. She did wrong. Go away, little boy, nasty boy, little lizard. Stamp him out. Turn away.

That was wrong. Where've you been? Let's see your hands. Go upstairs and wash them quick. What have you been up to? Saying nothing, not revealing that he knew, all the birds above laughing. But afterwards, whenever he hit her, riled beyond measure by anything little – answering back, perhaps, or getting in his way – it was for that he was beating her: dreadful sin, unspoken, hidden, like a worm in the belly, he was beating it out of her, her father, nettle-gatherer, punishing her skin with his stinging hands.

It was wrong. An inversion. The princess mustn't awake. Said the thirteenth fairy: the princess must die; and then the twelfth fairy spoke: I will lessen the spell; the princess will merely sleep. But only when it's a prince who comes breaking through the tangle may there be waking, and the forest put out flowers like blood.

The pastel plain is cold. In the distance the green meets stone-blue mountains. Someone comes. Hear him coming: the clatter of metal. See his armour wink in the sun. He stops, statuesque, surveys the scene, and the brooding forest. He lifts his arm, a stiff movement of iron. He holds up his sword of cold blue steel.

He always hurt her. The quick brush of an arm, the perfunctory kiss, her body claimed as his right, and then straight away his purple root thrusting, knocking over and over on the core of her belly. She would turn her head, close her eyes, disengage. Cut off her brain. Cut off its signals, make her abdomen numb. She never once had an orgasm with Roland. Roland her husband. Roland the professional. The straight man. The stiff man.

And yet she had needed him. His immobile face, his

puppet gestures, his solid silence – it was these she had needed. He was her wrapping-paper figure, he covered up the throbbing spaces of her sin.

Sinful pleasure. It was that she had had for a brief time with the other, her lover. It had to be paid for. She had to atone.

Twenty

THEY WILL PRESERVE the body. The body that she has renounced, they have infused. They have preserved it, improved it. They take care. They make checks. Temperature: normal. The substance in the veins has a regular pulse rate.

They unfasten the drip. The hand falls, bruised. They smile. It's nothing, the bruise will fade, soon there'll be nothing, only the slightest round white scar from the puncture. Everything soon will be good as new. Perfect.

They take precautions. 'You must get up, move about.' They must avoid the danger of leg thrombosis, a natural evil to be watched, wayward nature in the veins. They will beat it, out-trick it. 'You must get up.'

They will take her for a shower. They will clean the body, wash away the sweat of sleep and delirium. They unhook the bag of urine from its stand. They hold it while, unsteadily, she swings her legs off the bed. The tube, still attached to her bladder, threatens to tangle. The nurse pulls the bag away and releases it. They must help her now, she can't lift her own body, she can't yet rise across the barrier of pain. They tuck their arms about her, they lift together.

She stands. She sways. They encourage: 'That's right, come on. You'll be better for walking.' She takes a trembling step. Steady hands on her elbows.

'Here.' The one carrying the bag of urine holds it out to her.

'You'd better carry it yourself.'

She takes it. Plastic bag. The preserved contents of her own bladder. As she brings it closer, the tube, emerging from her own gown, pulls the hem up in folds.

They make their way from the room.

A cold draught blasts in the dimmer corridor. They shuffle slowly. They reach a lighted doorway. Zelda stops. She leans, resting. They wait. She looks up. Inside the doorway there's a screen, a large square monitor. Luminous dots pop up, swim across and disappear. She looks back at the nurses. She looks from one to the other.

'When will I get to see my baby?'

They look at her hard. They look at each other. 'You've seen him, haven't you?'

Oh, yes, of course. Seen an eye. No, two. Which was it? Which one do these two nurses think they have shown her?

'But when can I feed him?'

'Soon. You haven't been well. Soon. Don't worry.'

They shuffle on towards the shower. Now one of the nurses leaves. The other opens the door. She removes Zelda's gown. Up. Hold the bag with one hand; change over. Up the other side. Over her head. Her naked body. Swollen, stitched. Not functioning yet without external aids. Wash it down.

The nurse turns on the shower. Not too cold, not too hot; the body can't yet take too much shock. There, just right. She gently pushes her under. The water spatters, gathers, and streams.

'Here you are.' The nurse hands her a parcel. Something coloured. She holds it out, waiting. The water streams, licks down between the breasts and over the belly. What is it, what's she holding? Zelda peers, leaning closer to see, beginning to sway. It's her own. It's something she has owned. A bag, with fabric flowers. For use in a bathroom, containing the usual requisites for washing. Something she once used. Something from before. She stares, through the water.

'Here you are.' The nurse still holds it out, ready to exchange it for the one with Zelda's urine.

The water hisses; she moves her head. The water gurgles in her ears. 'Here you are.' Fish-voice bubbling.

'Are you all right?' asks the nurse, dropping the bag and leaning quickly forward.

'Here you are,' says the fish. 'This memory.'

They are going to the river. Someone is cooking. Marjoram is budding by the garden wall. The cookbook lies open on the kitchen table. Pots and pans clatter. The sounds of distant machines fly like torn paper. Inside someone is cooking a recipe for fish. The sound of sawing comes from the woodshed. A gleaming bowl of metal is placed on the doorstep: a colander of peas. The printed page lies open. Mother is cooking a dish fit for a king. The sound of Father's sawing stings. Fish with dill, the herb for lulling. A dish to soften and appease the king.

Father emerges from the woodshed. The sound of distant engines flies and falls, like birds. Father calls. Mother comes, head and shoulders to the window. The fish is left lying on the table, staring eye, split guts, white flesh prised open. Dead fish; who caught it? Distant men, on a boat with an engine. Father calls, emerges from the woodshed, whole body in the doorway. Mother answers, head and shoulders nodding: she can tell him, she's been watching, she knows the place where he left the thing he's lost. Father, appeased, disappears back into the woodshed. Wooden box. Inside he's sawing, white bones of wood amongst the kindling. The fish lies on the table, rainbow scales across its body. Engine sounds flutter in the distance like confetti. Fish-body lies on the table, dragged up through a wake of iridescent engine oil. Inside the shed, Father begins drilling. In the distance, the power station gathers, electrical and mechanical forces gather. The cookbook lies open.

Mother looks up from the window. Head and shoulders in the window. In the lane, beyond the wall, Hilary is waiting. Marjoram is budding by the garden wall. Marjoram for love. Hilary is waiting. Mother's white face flashes. Hilary is far too old to be waiting. Thirteen, too old. Thirteen unlucky. Mother's white face flashes. Where are they going? Don't go to the river.

They are going to the river. The cookbook lies open. They run. The birds fly up like shredded paper. The river wells, syrups around the blades of rushes. Electric forces gather. Boom of blasting, the puff of the genie. The river wells. It could flood. The fishes would escape, swim through the grasses, float in the tree-tops, come in under the eaves and whisper in your ear. The river wells. It pushes over their legs. Their arms bend in the water, and turn greenish-blue. The reeds sway, a black forest. The trunks move, glance together, unravel and tangle. A fish slips in like a shadow. It is feeding, nuzzling the succulent stems of the forest. Sun ripples, lights up its dappled belly. Her hands are white, palms upward. The fish moves above them. Its belly brushes her fingers. Her fingers move. The fish nudges. One flick, the fish goes flying, one quick flick of the hand, exactly timed, instinctive; the fish breaks through the water, cracks up, arcs through the air, spraying light like gravel, and lands, just on the bank.

The fish writhes. They churn out of the water. The fish catapults, gasps. She grabs, the fish slithers. For one moment she has it: head-on, its mouth wide, as though about to speak, and after all, from the front, two gleaming black eyes.

Twenty-one

How long has it been waiting in its transparent case? It is pink as wax. It is still. Its eyes are shut. Its life is closed inside. A label records the particulars of its existence: weight, method of delivery, the precise time of night it was born. Nurses, idling in slack moments, hang their bodies over the cot. 'Ooh, he's gorgeous,' they murmur. 'Isn't he?' they ask her, energetically.

They also ask, 'Are you all right?' Lingering, interested. To have fainted in the shower: that was proof, that was dramatic.

Yes, she's all right.

They smile, they hang on. This they can respect. Not pain, that's too familiar, the commonplace experience of it, but something much rarer, this thing they think they are seeing in Zelda: Transcendence. Bravery.

She makes to leave her bed. They hasten to help her. She calls sharply: 'I can manage!'

They falter. Are they wrong? Is it not bravery after all that they're seeing? Is it simply ungracious arrogance?

In the twilight corridor where Zelda goes alone, there are figures moving. They loom up, they pass, they shuffle on. The lavatory is engaged. Zelda waits in the yellow gloom of the bathroom. One light bulb has gone. It has not been replaced. It will not be replaced until the person whose job it will be to replace it is instructed to do so. No one else will replace it, that will not be allowed. There'd be a fuss, that kind of thing can end in a strike. Each must do only what they have been allocated.

She waits, holding her jug for collecting the urine and measuring its volume. The flush roars, the door latch clicks, the door winks: the occupant emerges. A tousled head, like dried grass, a rust-coloured dressing gown. The woman washes her hands wearily. She stands with them dripping. There are no paper towels; the roller is empty. It's the age of strikes, and shortages, and making do. The woman stands, her hands dripping, stuck out in front of her. She sways. She's so tired. Then she wipes them down the front of her mud-coloured cover. She shuffles out.

When Zelda comes out of the toilets, someone has switched the lights off in the corridor. Light shines out from the rooms and drops in bands along its length. She looks in as she passes. Interiors flash, surprising patchworks of colour: women, framed, caught in movement.

Then she stops. She knows this one. Inside the frame the light is dimmed. There is no human movement. The only things moving are the dots on the screen. On the bed lies a girl. Her pale arms are placed over the sheet. Her blonde hair is splayed on the pillow. Her eyelids are sealed. Zelda stares. The green dots jump on the screen, swim across, flicking tails, dive, submerge. The girl's hair fans on the pillow, shining and smooth. Someone has combed it over the pillow. Since it was combed, the girl has not moved. The arrangement stays perfect. Pre-Raphaelite princess. On the monitor, dots and dashes jump and fade, the flickerings of a soul.

'She lost her baby,' says a voice behind Zelda. She turns. It's the woman in the rust-coloured dressing gown. The woman leans her body on the doorframe.

'Oh,' says Zelda.

They stare in. It can happen. It could have happened.

It has happened to this girl. Death swimming up, snatching, flicking quickly back to the seabed.

'She's very ill,' says the woman, leaning beside Zelda. It has happened. Soul divided from body, reduced to luminous fish-dots, a lost genie shrivelled up inside a machine.

Zelda leans with the woman. They are so tired. Washed up, like fish. But they are breathing. They are lucky. The woman's eyes look out from her scarecrow head. Behind her mud-coloured wall she is a person, breathing.

From Zelda's room there come voices. The thirteenth room. Labelled fourteen; call it what you like, it's still the thirteenth room.

'Ooh,' comes a nurse's voice, 'he's the spitting image.'

'Isn't he?' she says to Zelda, as Zelda enters.

And there's someone else. Roland.

She's been waiting for Roland.

She says, 'Where've you been, Roland?'

Roland says, 'You have plenty of flowers.'

She looks around. Yes, so she has. And all the same. It must be because of the time of the year, the only flowers you can get, hothouse flowers. She says their name: 'They are Freesias.' She remembers. She knows it. She says to Roland, 'They are Freesias.' She tastes the name, round and round in her mouth; she turns to the nurse so she can say it again: 'Don't I have a lot of Freesias?'

Freesias. A new name. The old name with a different meaning. It was lost, it was divided from the bodies of the flowers. It comes back now with the meaning of that loss in its sound. She hisses it, 'Freesias,' and touches them lightly, red, yellow and blue ones. They bob, knock about in the vases, she spoils the arrangements. Who are they from? She might read the cards in the morning.

They think she's mad. They are looking uncomfortable,

the nurse and Roland. She stares back. The nurse shuffles, bustles out.

'Where've you been, Roland?'

'I came twice, but you were sleeping.'

'Ah. How are the roads?'

'Pretty bad. You know you can't cross the city now without the risk of driving into a sewer.'

'Uh-huh.'

Roland's ears are red with strain.

'What about the research, did you manage with that?'

'Oh, yes, it's done. It was difficult, though, this coming at the same time as the completion of the trial. Still, it's done.'

'Oh, good.'

'I don't know how, though, I wasn't there half the time.'

Sixty rats injected daily in their tails, every day caught and stabbed, rendered sterile when their backs were turned, revealing their secrets the first time Roland turned his.

'It's a good job,' he says, 'I can trust my technicians.'

It's all right, after all. The secrets are recorded, transformed first into chemicals and thence metamorphosed into clear authoritative print. The world, after all, will have Roland's findings on the contraceptive pill. It's all right, he can forget his difficulties, he can bury them.

'Where were you?'

He seems to gasp, his neck flushes red. 'Zelda, are you attacking me?'

'No, Roland,' she says.

'I kept coming,' he says, 'but you were asleep.'

He isn't taking any notice of the baby. But then neither is she. Perhaps he's suspecting she's an unnatural mother. The baby lies in its cot. Wheeled in an hour earlier. Labelled and packaged. What life has it led? In another stark place, fed efficiently by strangers, from a cold glass bottle. It is still.

It is closed on its small cold coil of experience. She hasn't fed it yet. She doesn't know its cry.

A nurse pops her head round. 'Baby still asleep, Mrs Harris? Don't forget to call when he wakes, we'll need to show you how to feed him. Ooh, isn't he a poppet?' she says, coming right in. 'Isn't he?' she darts, with an over-jolly tone, before she goes out again. This mother needs to be encouraged. This mother is not a caring mother.

Through the doorway the Sister and the houseman stand together talking. The houseman keeps swinging away and then turning back again. He keeps thinking of things to say. He doesn't go, he lingers.

'Have they done a ward round today?' asks Roland.

'Not that I know.' Perhaps they came when she went to the bathroom. Perhaps they missed her. She looks around the room, imagining it empty, just the bundle in the plastic cot. All around there are freesias. Waxy, artificial.

Roland says, 'You've not seen the Professor?'

'No.'

'I hear he's been away, but he's coming back today.'

No, she's not seen the Professor since she was in labour. He wasn't of course there at the birth. Zelda, having failed for so long to establish good strong labour, was not delivered until late evening, and then, naturally, by an emergency officer.

'Mm.' Roland looks slightly perturbed. Could it be seen as a professional slight, that the Professor has so arranged things that he's not been around? Or to put it less paranoiacally, that he has failed to arrange things so that he might be around? No, the suspicion is only momentary, Roland recovers. These things happen. You can't plan them. Roland buries his suspicion.

'Roland,' she says carefully, 'did he tell you they are doing this all the time now? Inducing, just for the sake of it, for no particular reason except that they think it's better? He told me.'

Roland's eyes slew. He stares hard. He looks right away. Is he shocked by a truth he hasn't suspected? Or is he caught out in a lie? Did he know all along, did the Professor let him into the secret from which she was excluded? His eyes shuttle, his thoughts tumble, revolve, then jackpot, he has it, the words which will appease her and prevent her from knowing.

'That's not what he said. Though I can see thinking back, that it could conceivably have been what he meant. He spoke of it as a precautionary measure.'

'But if it was commonplace, surely we'd have known about it, heard of it happening, read about it somewhere?'

'Well, I suppose it's one of these things that have been clinically proven, but are only just coming into general practice.'

She stares. He's justifying the system. If he didn't know he must have guessed. He buried the implications. The ins and outs didn't matter. He decided for her. She was his, claimed by right, to treat as he saw fit. She had no right to knowledge. That she had forfeited.

An eye for an eye. She had hurt him, she must pay. The one thing he hadn't buried. Not as she had – sewn it in, pretended none of it had happened, the secret meetings in hotels, the furtive phone calls, her nerves taut as the telegraph wires, the brief syrup of delirium welling in the pit of her longing, then the bile of her shame and Roland's hurt and disgust. She dug it over, dug it in, the face of the other.

It comes up now, a bland bubble. It floats away.

A gouged eye for an eye. One yawning space for another. A gap in her knowledge. She had forfeited insight.

She looks at Roland. He is tense. A small stiff man, head

round as a turnip, eyes two buttons, two dots of nostrils. His skin is red, over-coloured, over-exposed.

She was wrong. She was wrong all along. To expect this stiff person to cover her spaces. And that is something she has done herself, not just something that happened to her; her own error, her own act of blind faith. She appointed him as her saviour, prince hacking through the brambles, husband speeding through the rush-hour traffic. But what prince, hacking in the darkness, wouldn't be unnerved by the skulls already hanging in the branches, already picked clean?

It is something *she* has done to *him*: made him the victim of her expectations. And he could never match up. He might come, but all the time she stayed coldly asleep. In the cold glass case of her sleeping desires there wasn't really ever any room for Roland. And so there had been no room in her body.

And knowing this, all along, but pushing it under, she had shielded him from the truth of it. Dishonest. Unfair.

She won't do it any more. She says, moving round the end of the bed: 'If you think, Roland, the Professor was really implying that induction for its own sake is accepted and routine . . .' She pauses, to think clearly, and to let him dwell on what she's saying and understand all the implications. In the stillness, something moves inside the cot, a small section of the bundle nestling.

She goes on: 'Or if not, if you think he was saying mine had to be done for specific medical reasons . . .' She moves towards her locker '. . . then I think you should look at this.'

She bends, wincing over her stitches, and opens her locker. She brings out a slip of paper.

Roland's eyes pop. He flushes darker. 'Where did you get that?' Oh, how could she?

She says, 'I found it in my notes. They left the file beside my bed. Careless of them, wasn't it? *Anybody* could have picked them up. I rifled through them and took it out before they remembered, and came to fetch them.'

How could she? It isn't hers. Not *her* notes at all, whatever she calls them. Hospital property. Private information. Roland wouldn't like to think any patient of his had the nerve to do this. And she's the patient of the Professor. To be causing trouble, and be Roland's wife, and the patient of the Professor.

She holds the sheet towards him. A temperature chart, a record of contractions and the foetal heartbeat. She holds it out: pale, blue, criss-crossed with a webbing of squares. Hand-drawn threads and dots like mites scrawl up and down.

She points to the heading, in case he evades it. It is inked above her name:

Clinical Trial: Convenience Induction.

Twenty-two

THE PROFESSOR LIED to Roland. Or stretched the truth a bit. What does it matter, it will be a truth shortly – the Professor will make it one.

Even now, at the moment, he'll be holding an audience in the spell of his promise. He has sold his idea.

'What we have here, in effect, Ladies and Gentlemen, is the simple process of putting two and two together – or rather, even more simply, one and one: a uniparous birth to the mother of this invention.'

The audience titters.

'A simple logical connection, Ladies and Gentlemen, seemingly obvious once it has been made, but revolutionary in its practical implications, opening up hitherto unimagined possibilities on the obstetric ward.

'Take the oxytocin drip, something that has been with us for a good few years now. Add this new, highly sophisticated foetal monitor. And there we have it. A way to ensure the safety of all inductions. It is now conceivable that we could manage seventy-five per cent of uncomplicated pregnancies in this way, and so confine the main proportion of deliveries to the safety and convenience of the social hours.'

He draws to a close. The audience applauds. He raises his fingers like bloodless supermarket sausages. Question time. He draws his fingers through his hair. It sticks up, orange felt. He sways, a possible Aunt Sally.

Someone fires: 'Did you hint, Professor, that this technique has already been used for routine induction of normal healthy pregnancy?'

'Oh, yes. Indeed. We are using it ourselves with marked success. We have found it to be the best possible way to ensure the health of both the mother and the baby. It is a system, we have found, that works very well for the convenience of everyone.' (Except, in her case, it wasn't so convenient, as it turned out, for Roland.) 'It is possible to envisage a situation in the very near future when most deliveries will take place when the best available help is at hand.' (Except of course as in her case, when the patient fails to respond in time.)

Will take place, are already taking place, what does it matter? The Professor is no Aunt Sally, but a prophet: it will all be true soon, indeed, it's true already; the word is spoken and the truth created. Clinical Trial: just a term applied for the purpose of publishing papers. It is commonplace already, routine experience. The audience has faith in the truth of it, they're not gods, they need faith. Why, even the Professor needs something to worship: the perfect body nailed to the machine.

If Rick Jenkins, that inadequate student, ever gets as far as scanning the notes from the Professor's lecture, will he dare to see irony in what he has written under INDICATIONS FOR INDUCTION?:

NON-OBSTETRIC b) Administrative.

Would he dare be so profane? No irony is intended, that would spoil the satisfying pattern.

The Professor lied to Roland. Or stretched the truth a bit. Did Roland believe him, what did he believe of it? Roland is adjusting. Roland is feeling, on the whole, now he comes to think of it, seeing it in retrospect, that after all he knew, all along, in a way. Roland can't bear to think he's been lied to. The truth must take on the contours of his faith.

Burying the truth. The error she shared, in pretending she loved him. He sits, his back erect, his thick legs splayed. His hand on his knee is bent in at the wrist with a sudden sharp crease, as though it's stuck on haphazardly, anatomically incorrect, like the awkward drawing of a child. Roland as saviour. After all, that was just a figment of her imagination.

She would pity him no longer for the fact that, weak as he was, he couldn't be. She would patronise him no longer.

A nurse pops her head round. 'Mrs Harris? Could you stay in your room, please? We're expecting the Professor on a ward round any minute. Ooh, he's a bobby-dazzler,' she says, momentarily distracted. 'Isn't he?' Then she's gone.

'I must be going,' says Roland. He'll miss the Professor.

He kisses her briefly, a cold wet fish kiss. He's gone too, back across the crumbling sewers and the lit-up ribs of the city, the city to which he brought her in pursuit of his career.

Or perhaps – perhaps something else: perhaps, after all, the Professor didn't lie to Roland. Perhaps Roland understood, it was understood between them, the Professor and Roland, that he was stretching the truth a bit. If so, Roland, weak as he was, just wouldn't have had the guts to object. He'd be too scared to make a fuss . . . And something else: she remembers his state that night, his loss of confidence, his fear about his work . . . And suddenly she knows what it is that would have been at the core: Roland would have been too frightened for his own reputation to be obstructive with a superior, too afraid for his own professional future.

And he'd never have had the guts to admit as much to her.

Twenty-three

THE TRICK IS sorting out the stories. It isn't even a question of whether you believe them. Father hinted, rubbed his chin, and a picture was released: a misty plain of blue nettles, three black fir trees like arrows, a cool lake where the lost coins of fish lay flung at the bottom. The sisters wander away, fuzzed hair and swished dresses. Father stands alone and gathers for keeping the sharp essence of nettles.

With the same hands, he drew. She pushed the door of the cupboard under the stairs: as it shut, the roll glimmered. And she knew what they were, his drawings, threaded and faint and ringing her own. They were patterns, to be translated, into thick stone blocks, into concrete reality. They were plans for the power station. With his hands, he drew the plans, and the walled city grew up, gleaming white in the sunshine, a turreted castle. And poisonous dust dropped, seeping and burning the countryside all round.

She did wrong. He was displeased. He screwed up his mouth as though a black bitter sloe had shrivelled his tongue. He raised his hand with its scarred blood-brother thumb. When he beat her, his hands left the bright marks of nettles.

She'd done wrong. She had failed. And the paragon child smiled down, a reproach, sealed in Mother's memory, and expectations: paragon child-mother, her pocket money sensibly spent, perfect-toothed, taking a bite from the golden apple. But listen to the story: there's Grandmother calling – 'You'll get wind eating that, you'll fart the mattress off the bed!' Isn't she awful, isn't she crude, rattling coarsely through a set of false teeth – see, she ate too many sweets, she relished too many puddings, not a tooth to call her own, she's fat and indelicate and ugly and old.

Yet they laughed, she and Mother in the kitchen. Something was confused. Mother the cook caught out in a contradiction. Mother the conjuror caught out in uncertainty. Child-mother and child, it would happen to them: after lives of cooking, cooking and serving, they too would grow old. Was it fear that made them laugh, or was there something of relief?

To eat alone, to have it all to yourself, to shuffle carefree in the woods, to need no approval, to be free of the trap of the cold glass case. And to suffer no guilt. It was that, after all, that was the power of the witch. Merely that. All that.

They laughed, schizophrenic, caught between that truth and the pre-sealed images: mad, hysterical witch, apple sticking in the throat.

She can break the seal. She can make her own inversion. There's a movement in the cot, a small area struggling. A sound escapes, a little gasp. A nurse pops up: 'Ooh, he's getting hungry, isn't he? Just hang on, and we'll help you feed him when the Professor's been in!'

There's a bustling in the corridor, a jumping to attention, Sister Barbara and Houseman Andrew shuffling off their lascivious languor, Andrew immediately stiff with deference, though poised to display his own clinical acumen. They'll be tingling, both of them, with the excitement of pretence, perhaps exchanging furtive glances as the Professor bends to feel a bloated fundus, wrapped up in themselves, too distracted for empathy.

Another madness. To have allowed herself into a position where her only recourse would be the empathy of others.

It falls quiet in the corridor. The entourage has started two rooms along. There will be time. She moves toward the cot. She leans over, and for the first time now she looks in at the bundle. Amongst the swaddling, fingers wriggle, breaking out; the face, screwed, emits small tearing sounds. The arms make sharp convulsions: the wrapping falls open, the arrangement is broken.

She hears them coming along the corridor, their voices reverent and low, the givers of life according to their own strict patterns. False patterns. Their gods are false: their stiff patterns can fail them. Death can leap up from the depths, gobbling, jump back into the machine; electric grids across the land, sustenance and life meted out in geometric patterns: the lights could go out, the machines fail at any moment, a troll can jump down from industrial scaffolding, stalk a child in the woods and smash its skull.

The head, a dusky lozenge. She leans over. She raises her hands. She reaches into the cot. Touches the cold white lump of the body. Takes hold and lifts.

Across the room, quickly. Stop in the doorway. Listen. The voices are muffled, in the next room. Which way? Turn right, that's it. Double doors. She tightens her grip, and flinching over her stomach, takes the weight of the door. A cold lighted space of open corridor. At the end, the butt of the staircase, the way to the outside world and freedom. She listens again. Someone is coming up the stairs. She looks around in panic. There's a door on the right: she slips in, and shuts it behind her.

The light is dim. Slowly her eyes become accustomed. There's a sink, and coats hanging. Nurses' cloaks: this is the staff cloakroom and lavatory. The outer door has a lock; there it is, a metal twist. She turns it full circle.

The baby is silent. It has stopped its gasping whimpers.

Its eyes are wide open. Two dark eyes, all wide pupils. The baby stares. Listening. Waiting. So here it is. Here it is in her hands, large hands for a woman, the thing that was sown and immediately buried. Buried too deep, and never acknowledged. She stares. The baby waits, its eyes wide open, receptive.

She hears their voices through the doors: 'Where's Mrs Harris? I told her to stay there –' She imagines her room. The sheet rolled back, the plastic cot empty, just the cut heads of flowers from unidentified senders. She names them: 'Freesias.' She names the birds – starlings, and seagulls, she gives them all back their names, new names, the old names with different meanings; and the fish – the silver perch that jumped, the waiting pike and the nuzzling trout.

She names herself: Teacher, Scientist. The words taste. At last they have texture. At last, to acknowledge her own insights, to be her own author.

She knows how the medical staff will be standing, looking into the empty room, she can visualise their irritation as they search the patients' toilets. They'll be annoyed, but not worried, they have too much faith in their system to imagine the possibility: Ladies and Gentleman, my last trick but one, the disappearing trick. She begins to laugh. Silently, she shakes. It hurts, her stitches strain, she holds the baby against them to ease them, and then she's laughing to split her guts, holding them in with the bundle of the baby. The baby nestles his warm head against her vibrating body, his mouth begins to search.

She holds him off, there's no time. Soon, baby, soon. She puts him down and works quickly. She peels off her nightgown and riffles through the clothes hanging on the wall. A grey dress, that will do. A roomy nurse's cloak. She's dressed: now it's time. Ladies and Gentlemen, and now for the last trick. Metamorphosis.

She untwists the door lock. She listens. Silence. No one

about. She steps out, the baby hidden under the cloak. She starts off towards the stairs, her slippers clack on the floor and echo off the empty walls. She's on the stairs: open-railed, airy, unpeopled; the upper floor drops away and back, a receding spaceship. Across the foyer where figures drift, benignly strange, unconcerned, and letting her pass. And then outside. The cold air hits her lungs and lifts the cloak like wings. She waves; a taxi skims towards her. She knows now where'll she'll go, not to Roland, nor the other, they are two grown men, they don't have to need her.

The baby moves beneath the cloak. He doesn't cry. She moves the cloth aside: his eyes are wide open, waiting for her, waiting for images.

She shuts the door. The taxi moves. They are safely away.

Author's Note

IN SPITE OF the 'death of the author', no novel gets written without a novelist's strong intention, and my intention when I wrote *The Birth Machine* in 1982 was to tell a story exploring the hubris of much contemporary 'scientific' thinking. In particular, I was interested in the contemporary tendency to overlook, or even deny, the factor of uncertainty. In the background were the pronouncements of politicians and 'scientists' with vested interests that there was no proof of any link between the nuclear power station at Sellafield and the cancer clusters nearby – overlooking the point that there was no proof of no link, either – and their conclusion that *therefore we could be confident that there was no danger*, rather than the more logical one that we could not make any pronouncements about the level or likelihood of danger, and therefore ought to be careful, in case (a lack of logic applied later to BSE); the arrogance of the nuclear industry in general and of the space race (the Chernobyl and Challenger disasters waiting to happen); travesties like Thalidomide already acknowledged in our socio-pharmacological history.

Obstetrics was especially apt as a context for my theme: it is in the moments of birth that the line between burgeoning life and proximate death is at its fuzziest, and, in the contemporary high-tech set-up, so-called scientific objectivity and personal subjectivity most strikingly in conflict.

The original version of *The Birth Machine*, as it appears in this edition, is specifically structured to establish, in the opening chapters, the last of these concerns – the problematic conflict between scientific 'objectivity' and personal subjectivity. Chapter One begins with the famous Professor, the supposed carrier of scientific objectivity, addressing a conference. The setting is deliberately international, far removed in geography and glamour from the hospital bed to which we will eventually be taken. We witness the effect of the Professor's charisma, and thus his influence; we follow briefly his hectic dash back across the Atlantic, his lordly sweep through his secretary's office and on to the ward where the students await him. The woman on the bed is seen by us through the eyes of the students, as an object in his virtuoso demonstration. While the whole is undercut by satire, and a questioning of the authority of the Professor thus prompted, the only world we are in any way invited to share is that of the medical profession, and the very mode of satire implicates the reader in a stance of superiority and detachment.

At the end of Chapter One a new viewpoint and tone are signalled, and the opening of Chapter Two takes us into a contrasting world: the childhood memories of Zelda, the woman lying on the bed – triggered, ironically, by the way the nurses treat her like a child.

But this is yet another displacement. It is not until Chapter Four that we are presented with the cold reality of Zelda's subjective experience of the initial procedures of obstetric induction.

This structure is intended to wean the reader (and *in particular* the unwilling or squeamish reader) gradually from the safety of 'objectivity', via a growing familiarity with Zelda through her memories, to the shock of her subjectivity – though even then her experience is presented as flashback, in third-person past tense: Zelda herself, leave alone the reader, can only contemplate it at a distance. There is a further, more important, intention: to demonstrate, via these perspective shifts, the shocking temptations for all of us in the glamour of detachment.

Katy Campbell, reviewing the first edition in *City Limits*, declared the book 'especially recommended for anyone involved in the Obstetrics industry.' Since Obstetrics was (and still is) dominated by men, it is ironic, therefore, that the publisher prepared in 1983 to take on such a novel was publishing for women. For The Women's Press edition, the chapter confronting us with Zelda's subjective experience (here appearing as Chapter Four) was moved to the beginning. Since readers were not expected to be male, the suasive tactics of my earlier structure were judged unnecessary, and a beginning with which women readers could identify was thought more desirable. This change necessitated, structurally, another change: from past to present tense within the chapter, increasing further its immediacy.

In the end it's not for me, as the writer, to say which version is *better*, or whether either version fulfils completely the authorial/editorial intention behind its creation, and whether indeed it matters if it doesn't – all this has to be up to readers. I do believe, however, that they are different books, with different meanings. What we read first in any piece of work filters what we read next (however differently each maverick reader reads), and I believe that the placing of the 'subjective' and non-satiric chapter at the start lent the whole a realist and 'confessional' slant, and it was this which prompted readings of the novel as a passionate plea for natural childbirth, rather than as the plea for logic I intend it to be.

ELIZABETH BAINES

Lightning Source UK Ltd.
Milton Keynes UK
UKHW041237130921
390500UK00003B/506